Praise for *Pageant*

"The first charm of *Pageant* is its healthy serving of early nineties nostalgia—so many beloved memories returned as I read. I also loved its focus on a deep and meaningful mother-daughter bond, as well as its explosive finale!"

-Christi Nogle, Bram Stoker Award® winning author of *Beulah*

"Wendy Dalrymple is en pointe with *Pageant*, a wicked little dance number that keeps the tempo building up until its gloriously gory crescendo."

-Brian McAuley, author of *Candy Cane Kills* and
Curse of the Reaper

"*Pageant* upholds Wendy Dalrymple's reputation for fun, accessible and imminently enjoyable storytelling. Tiffany, Dalrymple's nine year old narrator, is both lovable and believable, conveying her joy, fears and misgivings with poignant proficiency, and the supporting cast of characters fleshes the story out nicely. Perfect pacing and a satisfying plot combine with truly frightening and horrific elements to make *Pageant* another must-read for horror lovers."

-Laurel Hightower, author of *Below* and
The Day of the Door

"In *Pageant*, Wendy Dalrymple gives the reader a glimpse into the subtle and not-so-subtle violence of girlhood. Dealing with issues like body image, class disparities, and being an outsider, this is fast-paced pink horror with heart!"

-Tiffany Morris, Shirley Jackson Award nominee and
author of *Green Fuse Burning*

"At first glance, Wendy Darymple's *Pageant* seems like a glittery, coming-of-age story featuring sweet Floridian girls honing their talents and chasing the thrill of the stage. But if you sit in the front row...crane your neck just so ... and peer beyond the 90s neon spandex ... you'll get the chance to witness so much more. Little-girl rage, the unattainable pursuit of perfection, the realization that the world is full of both bad actors and found family, and ... blood. Lots and lots of blood.

"The girls are backstage. The lights are dimming. Are you ready for the show?"

-Tiffany Michelle Brown, Author of
How Lovely to Be a Women: Stories and Poems,
Co-host of the Horror in the Margins podcast

"Dalrymple uses the bright and often sparkly world of pageants to tell a haunting story of what happens when someone is stripped of their individuality and forced to conform to a system that doesn't view them as human."

-Damien Casey, author of *Church of Skatan*

PAGEANT

Wendy Dalrymple

MADAXEMEDIA.COM

Published by Mad Axe Media

madaxemedia.com

Edited by Candace Nola

Book Cover by Joey Powell

Print ISBN: 979-8-9906858-8-8

E-Book ISBN: 979-8-9906858-9-5

Content Warnings for child abuse, food, eating disorders, suicidal ideation, murder, gore.

To Laura and Kevin Owen

Thank you for supporting all of my sparkle motion dreams.

Chapter One

"Tiffany Baldwin, you put that down *now*!"

Miss Suzy glared at me from across the dance studio floor, her hands propped up on her hips and balled into tight fists. A dozen pairs of eyes followed her pinched, angry gaze as everyone's attention focused squarely on me. My face grew hot as the entire dance class paused, and for a moment, all the air was sucked out of the room. I'd been caught. Miss Suzy's wave bangs bobbed back and forth in slow motion as she shook her head at me in a disapproving manner, but her sky-high hair sculpture did not budge. Miss Suzy was a first-rate artist when it came to crafting stage-ready hairdos and Aquanet was her favorite medium.

I stared down at the brand new black and white cake in my hand as its soft, pillowy filling encased in a waxy white and black fondant called to me. I hadn't eaten anything all day except for water, baby carrots, celery sticks, and plain boiled chicken and I. Was. STARVING. I just needed a little pick-me-up before tap class began, but obviously, Miss Suzy didn't understand. I frowned, wrapped the cakes back in their cellophane wrapper, and stuffed them into my gym bag. They would taste better during water break, anyway.

"Okay, now girls, this routine needs to be perfect for the Festival of Lights!" Miss Suzy tore her glare away from me and turned to the giant black stereo system at the front of the dance studio. "I wanna see big smiles and lots of energy!"

I hoisted myself up from the sidelines, picked the leotard out of my butt, and took my position next to Lisa. I was stuck at the back of the class, where Miss Suzy placed all the bigger, older girls. But even though I was hidden behind a sea of smiling faces, that didn't mean I wasn't going to do my best. I had been practicing the group tap routine for the last two weeks and knew every step-ball-change and shuffle step by heart. I held my breath as Miss Suzy placed the cassette in the stereo system and the intro to C+C Music Factory's *Gonna Make You Sweat* boomed through the studio.

The slap of dozens of tapping feet crashed in the air as we shuffled along to the song in perfect synchronicity. I focused on my form in the wall-to-wall mirrors as I tapped and posed to the choreographed electronic dance song. *Chin up, shoulders back, tummy tucked in, smile, smile, smile.* My chipmunk-cheeked reflection beamed back at me as I hit every single mark on time. It was true that I wasn't as cute and little as I used to be, but I was still a good dancer. Tap and ballet made me feel alive, and I wasn't ever going to stop dancing, even if I didn't look like the other girls. I could still do everything that the younger, smaller girls could do, but soon it wouldn't matter anymore. I was almost ten and Momma said that I probably wasn't going to be able to compete in kids' pageants anymore. Maybe that wouldn't be such a bad thing.

"Samantha, pick up your feet!" Miss. Suzy clapped her hands at the newest little girl in class. Samantha was only five, the youngest and smallest of us all, and as a result, she had been placed front and center. Her French braid was pulled so tight at her temples it almost looked painful. As Miss Suzy approached, Samantha stopped tapping and her pixie-ish features crumpled in the mirror. Big tears welled up in her eyes as our dance teacher and pageant director loomed over the exhausted and scared little girl.

"Go take a break, Samantha." Miss Suzy rolled her eyes and pointed toward the far end of the studio. "Come on girls, I need *energy*!"

My legs grew numb and tingly as Miss Suzy continued to yell and clap at the slower younger girls. I used to love coming to dance class and competing in pageants, but with every passing year, the whole thing began to make me sick. Momma said I should count myself lucky, though. Suzy Dawn Dance Studio was the premier place to be for every young girl in Southwest Florida who wanted to learn dance and compete in the pageant circuit. Momma started me in classes when I was only four, and that was the first year I competed as well. I won nine regional titles that year, and twelve the year after that. I even made the front page of the News-Press the year I turned six. Last year, I only won two trophies, and they were both for participation. This year, I probably won't win anything at all.

We worked harder and longer than usual on our group tap routine that evening. The Pageant of Lights was only three days away and the high-energy group tap routine was to be the opening number for the holiday show. It was called the Pageant of Lights, of course, because of our town's most famous former winter resident, Thomas Edison, and also because the pageant was happening around Christmas and Hanukkah. All of us girls were expected to learn and perform the choreographed group opening number, as well as our own evening gown interviews and the talent portion of the competition. Momma got me a really pretty dress for my interview portion in green velvet and lace to complement my naturally curly red hair. She told me I should talk about computers for the interview part because that would make me sound smart. I was to sing *Have Yourself a Merry Little Christmas* for my talent portion, but that's not what I really wanted to do. I wanted to dress myself up to look like a human Christmas tree and sing and tap to my favorite song, but Miss Suzy thought that was weird and told me just to sing instead.

We must have gone over our tap routine for *Gonna Make You Sweat* a dozen times before Miss Suzy was finally satisfied enough to let us take a water break. I wiped the moisture from my forehead, my heart beating fast as I collapsed on the sidelines next to my gym bag. Samantha sat down next to me, her eyes already welled up with tears, either from her too-tight braid, from Miss Suzy yelling at her or both. It hurt my heart to watch her look so sad. I didn't have any brothers or sisters, but at that moment, I wanted to protect her like she was my own little sibling.

"Want a snack?" I dug the opened package out of my bag and extended it toward the teary-eyed little girl.

Samantha nodded and sniffed. She took one of the hexagon-shaped treats and gave me a half-smile. We sat there together, watching the other girls talk and stretch as we ate the black and white cakes in silence, the thick vanilla frosting coating the inside of my mouth and soothing my soul all at once. If love had a taste, I think it would be cake.

"What are you doing for the talent competition?" I asked, brushing crumbs off my leotard.

"Baton twirling," she said, her voice barely a whisper.

"That's a good one," I said. "I wanted to dress up like a giant Christmas tree and sing *Jingle Bell Rock*, but Miss Suzy didn't like that idea."

"That would have been funny," Samantha said with a hint of a giggle.

"See! That's what I thought too." I gave her an encouraging smile. "How do you like dance class?"

"It's hard," she said, taking a bite of her cake.

"Don't worry, this all gets better. You're really pretty too, so I'm sure you'll win a lot of trophies."

"I don't want to win any trophies," she said. "I don't even like to sing and dance."

"Then why are you here?"

"My grandma made me. She says I have to come to class because she doesn't have time to sit around and take care of me all day."

"Your grandma sounds mean," I said.

"She is."

"Why don't you tell your mom and dad that you don't wanna go to class?"

Samantha sighed. "They died when I was a baby."

"Oh." A gross, barfy flavor filled my mouth. I was so dumb. Poor little Samantha was already having a bad day, and I just made it worse by opening my big mouth. "I'm sorry."

"It's okay." Samantha stood up. "I think we have to go back now."

She was right. The other girls were already lined up again. Miss Suzy glared daggers at me as I wiped cake crumbs from my chest. Panic spiked in my veins as I hoisted myself off the floor and scrambled to take my place in line.

"I'm coming!"

It was dark by the time class let out later that night and I was hungry again. I shivered as a cool breeze hit the back of my sweaty neck and I was glad that I had remembered to bring my white faux fur jacket. In Florida, people don't get a lot of chances to wear heavy coats 'cause it never really gets all that cold. Momma was smart and got me the coziest jacket on clearance last year after winter, and I'm glad she did, otherwise, I would freeze. Miss Suzy locked the doors after class so I had to sit outside as all the other girls from class filed into their parents' Buick's and BMW's and drove away. After a while, it was just Samantha and me left waiting on the bench outside Suzy Dawn Dance Studio staring out at the night.

"Is someone coming to pick you up?" I glanced down at Samantha. She was shivering too and didn't have a coat.

"Mhmm."

"Here." I took off my coat and wrapped it around her shoulders.

"Thanks." She let out a groan and cuddled into my coat. "I hate dance class."

"It's not always like this," I said. "Miss Suzy is tough on us, but that's only 'cause she wants us to win."

"Okay." Samantha shrugged. We sat there for another long stretch of silence, staring out into the woods that lined the parking lot. A blast of arctic air blew across my bare arms as a pair of headlights flashed in the parking lot. Samantha's body went rigid and a blue van with brown side panels pulled up.

"That's my ride." She slipped out of my coat and handed it to me. "Thanks for being so nice to me."

"See you tomorrow."

The passenger window of the blue and brown van rolled down and loud, angry-sounding music poured from the speakers. I tried to make out who was behind the wheel, but all I could see was the orange glow of a lit cigarette.

"Hurry the fuck up, Samantha!" A man's voice roared over the music.

Her expression paled as she glanced back at me with wide eyes. "I gotta go."

Heat crept up my neck and into my cheeks as I watched Samantha open the door and climb up into the van. I could feel the blood in my veins get all hot and bubbly, sloshing around inside of me like volcano lava or something. My teeth ground together, and my fists balled up tight, just like Miss Suzy's as the van screeched away.

That's when I got my first headache.

It began like a dull, sharp pain, kind of like when you eat ice cream too fast. But the pain didn't go away. It just kept spreading and growing, flowing from a spot right between my eyes, down into my neck and my arms, and all the way to my toes. I wanted to reach into the night and snatch little Samantha out of that horrible van and away from whoever it was that picked her up. I was so mad, so freaking *angry*! I stared up at the parking lot pole light and all I could see was red, red, red. I stared at that light for a long time until my eyes burned and the spot between my eyes throbbed.

Finally, when I couldn't take it anymore, I looked away and the light bulb flickered. A flash of color arced through the air, creating a zapping noise. The light bulb popped and exploded, spraying out sparkles of electricity like a firework. I jumped, and a scream ripped from my lungs. After a moment, the parking lot light fizzled and died, and I was surrounded by darkness.

My face burned as I struggled to catch my breath, panting as though I had just tap-danced for a mile. My heart beat so fast, but the headache disappeared as quickly as it had come on. Another rush of wintry air blew into the darkened parking lot, and I shrugged into my jacket, the lining still warm from Samantha's body.

That's when I spotted the flashing eyes.

My stomach dropped as I fixed my gaze toward the far end of the parking lot where the asphalt met the treeline, directly into the cat-like stare. The eyes staring back at me almost glowed in the dark like some kind of Halloween decoration. My lungs hurt, but I was too afraid to breathe, too afraid to move or even make a sound. Whatever it was that those eyes belonged to, I didn't want it to see me. I stayed as still as possible, hoping that I was hidden in the shadows.

After what felt like forever, a pair of headlights pulled into the parking lot. My heart leapt into my throat as Momma's blue Toyota rounded the corner. I glanced back toward the treeline to see if the eyes were still there, but I saw only shadows. I didn't know whether to be scared or relieved that whatever had been watching me was gone.

Momma rolled down the passenger window and called out to me as Fleetwood Mac's *Rhiannon* poured from the speakers.

"Tiffany, baby, I'm so sorry I'm late! My boss was being a jerk and made me refold all the shirts in the front lobby."

I swallowed the lump in my throat and forced my dead legs to move. I couldn't run very fast, but I didn't want whatever was in the woods to get me. I pushed myself off the bench, grabbed my gym bag, and made a beeline for the car. Momma looked like an angel behind the wheel as I opened the passenger door, her bouffant of red hair encircling her head like a fiery halo in the overhead light.

"Mom!" I let out a sob as I leapt into the front seat, clutching my gym bag to my chest. I shut the car door, slapped the lock, and rolled up the window as fast as I could.

"Tiffany! What's the matter?"

"I just wanna go home," I said, my voice a whimper.

"Alright." Momma threw the car into drive and gave me a concerned sideways glance. "Everything okay?"

"Yeah." I lied.

"Okay," she said, her voice tinged with doubt. "You want Micky D's for dinner?"

I nodded.

"You got it, babe." Momma leaned over and ruffled my bangs. "It's so *dark*. What the heck happened to the parking lot light?"

Chapter Two

If there's one thing my mother knew, it was how to make a dollar holler. Momma had a variety of tips and tricks on how to save money, and one of those ways was knowing every free kids' meal and coupon night at our favorite restaurants. On Wednesday nights after dance practice, we would always drive through McDonald's and stock up on .39 cheeseburgers. We would each have two cheeseburgers on the way home from practice and then save the rest in the fridge for lunch or dinner the next day. They didn't taste as good after you microwaved them, but leftover .39 cheeseburgers were better than nothin'.

By the time I finished my first cheeseburger, I had nearly forgotten about the busted parking lot light and the staring eyes. I didn't even think about sad little Samantha or the upcoming Festival of Lights. All I knew was the warm safety of my mother's car, the scent of her Exclamation! perfume and Stevie Nicks' voice floating through the stereo. By the time we reached Country View Estates, my second cheeseburger was gone, my belly was full, and my head and heart were almost right again.

Country View Estates was where me and Momma lived, but there was no view of the country, and our apartment complex sure wasn't any kind of estate. I knew we were poor — poorer than most of the other girls in the pageant circuit anyway — but we knew how to manage. Momma's job at the men's store in the mall brought in just enough money to put gas in the car and pay the rent on our one-bedroom apartment, but we had to "fill in the gaps" in creative ways. Food banks helped out with the groceries, but they were never enough to get through the month. Some kids teased me once about being on welfare, so I asked Momma about it, but she said we were too proud to take money from those who needed it more than us. Still, I had everything I could ever want and me and Momma were happy. Most of the time, anyway.

Competing in pageants was hard work, and it was expensive, but Momma had tons of tricks for making what little money we had stretch. She got all of my pageant clothes from the mall with her discount, and she learned how to do my hair and makeup real good. She even bartered with Miss Suzy and cleaned the dance studio and the bathrooms from top to bottom once a week in exchange for my lessons. I love my Momma. She would do just about anything for me and I would do just about anything for her.

I huffed up the stairs toward our apartment that night, exhausted from dance class and weighed down by a belly full of greasy, delicious cheeseburgers. I went straight to the bathroom, peeled off my sweaty tights and leotard, and showered with my favorite strawberry essence shampoo and conditioner. I didn't have school in the morning because we were already on Christmas break, but I still had to get clean anyway because Momma was taking me to work with her the next day. Whenever I didn't have school or dance and Momma had to work, she took me to the mall and let me roam around wherever I wanted, so she didn't have to pay a babysitter. See? I told you we knew how to make a dollar holler.

After my shower, I changed into my Garfield pajamas and went into the living room where Momma was already sawin' logs on the couch. An old black and white Christmas movie played on the TV, but I grabbed the remote and changed it to 'Nick at Night'. We got free cable too thanks to one of Momma's old boyfriends who was too lazy to disconnect our service after they broke up. I snuggled into the couch next to her, still warm from my shower, and bathed in the light of the little tabletop Christmas tree in the window. It was the same tree we had every year, our Charlie Brown Christmas tree, Momma called it. I decorated it with all the ornaments I made in art class each year, plus a box of candy canes we got from the dollar store. I reached over, grabbed one of the candy canes and unwrapped it, and began to zone out to an episode of *Bewitched*.

As I watched the lady on TV wiggle her nose and make stuff move around her house, I thought about the exploded parking lot light. I rubbed the spot in between my eyebrows, remembering how bad my head hurt after class. I considered telling Momma about the headache, but I didn't want to make her worry because doctors' appointments were expensive. She probably wouldn't believe me about what I saw in the parking lot, anyway. Maybe the eyes I saw along the treeline were just from some stray cat, or floaters from staring at the parking lot light for too long. There had to be some kind of explanation, right?

I pondered what had happened that night at Suzy Dawn Dance Studio and sucked on my candy cane until the end was pointed like a sword. I poked the pointy end of the candy cane into the tip of my finger, admiring how sharp I managed to get it. That's when the pain in my forehead returned. It was dull at first, then the further I pushed the candy cane sword into my finger, the more intense the headache throbbed. I pushed the point of the candy cane deep into the pad of my finger until it nearly bled, the pain in my head intensifying the further I dug in. I released the candy cane just before the sharpened tip broke through the skin and the pain in my forehead stopped.

I put the candy cane down on the coffee table, breathing hard. Something wasn't right. I glanced over at Momma. She was still fast asleep. I wanted to wake her and talk to her about what was happening, but I knew she was tired and needed to rest. I covered her with a blanket, turned off the TV, and tucked myself in bed. That night, I stared at the *90210* poster of Jason Priestly that hung on the ceiling over my bed until I was finally sleepy, and I couldn't think about glow-in-the-dark eyes or headaches or pageants anymore.

"Tiffany! Breakfast!"

The smell of flaky, toasted pastries filled my nostrils as my eyes popped open the following morning. I knew that smell well, frozen toaster pastries. My favorite. I threw off my kitten print comforter, swung my legs over the edge of my bed, and headed out the bedroom door and into the kitchen/living room. Momma was nice and gave me the only bedroom in our apartment. We had to share the closet, but still, I felt bad that she had to sleep on the couch.

"Good morning." Momma placed a plate of toasted strawberry pastries in front of me.

I grabbed the icing packets and began to drizzle each pastry with artistic flair. "Morning."

Momma took a sip of coffee. "You gonna see Santa at the mall today?"

I shrugged. "I guess."

"Are you getting too old for Santa?"

"No one is too old for Santa."

"That's my girl." Mom patted my back. "I'm going to go get ready for work. Can you be ready to go in about an hour?"

"Sure."

Momma disappeared into the bathroom as I ate my breakfast at the kitchen counter. I chewed slowly and thoughtfully because the frosted pastries would be my only treat of the day. Miss Suzy wanted us to eat a "healthy" diet and cheeseburgers and sweets weren't part of it. All of us girls at the dance studio were encouraged to eat less than what I usually like to eat, but I was so hungry all the time, especially after class. Momma didn't like that Miss Suzy tried to get us to follow what she called a "starvation" diet. She told me to just ignore what Miss Suzy had to say about diets and food and that it was still okay for me to have a few treats. I still tried to eat healthy anyway because I wanted to be a good dancer, but it was too hard to be perfect all the time.

By nine o'clock, Momma was out of the shower and dressed in her blue skirt suit, the one that I liked the best. Her hair was all fluffed up, and she had her work makeup done and she smelled nice. Momma was so pretty and elegant, and I hoped that I could be like her someday. She grabbed her purse, and I grabbed my gym bag, and we headed out the door into a crisp December morning.

"Now, I'm going to take you to Suzy Dawn's on my lunch break," Momma said as I hopped into the passenger seat. "I might be a little late picking you up again tonight."

I frowned and clicked my seatbelt. "Do I have to go then?"

Momma started up the car and gave me a funny look. "Why? Something bothering you?"

"I get nervous waiting outside," I said. "It was really dark last night, and I was all alone."

"Doesn't Miss Suzy let you wait inside the building?"

"No." I shook my head. "She lets us out and locks the front door."

"I don't like the sound of that. I'm gonna have a word with her." Momma grumbled, pulling out of our apartment complex. "I'll try to get out of work a little early to pick you up on time, then."

"Okay." I sighed and stared out the window. I felt bad. Momma worked hard so that I could take classes and compete. It would hurt her feelings if I wanted to quit. Still, the idea of continuing to go to Miss Suzy's classes made me feel sick, and I didn't want to get another weird headache. I didn't know what to do. Momma put in her Amy Grant Christmas album, and I relaxed a little as we drove toward the mall.

"Are you excited for Christmas?" Momma asked.

"Mhmm."

"What are you going to ask Santa for?"

I shrugged. "Roller skates. Probably some more painting stuff. And books, of course."

"That sounds good."

We listened to Amy Grant sing about Christmas and Tennessee and snow all the rest of the way to the mall. I had never seen snow, and I always wondered what it would be like to have a white Christmas. Maybe someday I would be able to leave Florida and find out.

Momma pulled into the Metro Mall parking lot just before 9:30 A.M. Her store didn't open until ten, but there were always customers there waiting outside the stores for the mall to open. The mall was extra busy that time of year and was beautifully decorated for the holidays. Seniors always came early to walk with their friends and "get their steps in". Me and Momma took the employee entry on the side of the building and a thrill went up my spine. It always felt cool to follow her into work, like we were doing something secret and special by walking through the back halls.

"Meet me at the Food Court around two. We'll get lunch before I take you to Miss Suzy's," Momma said, pulling out her employee name tag. MIRANDA BALDWIN was imprinted on a silver placket, her name shining in the fluorescent overhead lights.

My ears perked up at the mention of lunch. Momma's newest boyfriend, Tony, was the food court manager, and he let us eat from the salad bar for free. "Can we get big salads?"

"Yes, but not until Tony is on the clock." Momma kissed me on the cheek. "Be good. Come see me if you need anything."

"I will."

I hitched my gym bag over my shoulder and took off towards my favorite place in the mall. I passed the Santa's Village area in front of Burdines but kept going, the line already full of mothers with their toddlers all dressed in fussy Christmas outfits. The truth was that I was too old for Santa, but I didn't want to tell Momma that. It would only disappoint her.

I took my time walking through the mall towards Waldenbooks because I knew they wouldn't be open just yet. It was neat to be able to walk through the mall and look at all the stores, but it was also kind of sad in a way. Momma and I couldn't really afford to shop at most of the places unless she was friends with one of the people that worked there. I was glad Momma made friends with Judy, the bookstore manager. Judy would let me read so long as I didn't crack the spines of the books. Most of the time I read Nancy Drew or the latest Fear Street, but that day, I had another agenda.

"Good morning, Tiffany." Judy waved to me as she raised the gate over Waldenbooks. Judy was a really nice lady with short gray hair who wore fun sweaters and always seemed to be working. Sometimes she even brought me snacks or little presents. She was the kind of lady I wish I had for a grandma.

"Morning, Judy."

"You all ready for your big pageant?"

"Almost." I pouted. "I won't get to dress up like a Christmas tree, though."

"That's too bad," Judy said. "I know what would cheer you up, though. We just got a new Lois Lowry book in stock."

"That's okay," I said. "I have some research to do."

"For school?"

I paused for a moment. "Yeah."

"Okay, sweetie. Just remember to clean up after yourself."

"I will."

I glanced over my shoulder as Judy returned behind the register. We were lucky to have such a big bookstore at our mall. I could get lost in the aisles forever. I would have loved to go to a real library, but the only one in town was too far away and Momma couldn't waste the gas, so Waldenbooks was my library. Usually, I went straight to the Young Adult section, but today, I was strictly on the hunt for non-fiction.

I walked past Religion and History and turned toward the New Age/Occult section. The books in this section always looked so interesting to me, especially the ones with black leather-bound covers decorated with pictures of skulls and pentagrams and stuff. I didn't know what I was looking for in that section, only that I wanted some answers, and I knew I wasn't going to find them in the other aisles. There was a word that I was looking for to describe what I thought might be going on, and I couldn't remember it until I scanned some of the titles.

Telekinesis For Beginners

Telekinesis. That was it. I grabbed the thick textbook and also picked up a book on witchcraft just in case and headed to one of the reading tables. I had four hours to kill and lots of studying to do.

I pulled my Trapper Keeper out of my gym bag and opened it to my favorite kitten Lisa Frank notebook that I save just for special occasions. I grabbed a purple gel pen and got to work.

Tiffany Baldwin

December 16, 1993

　1. *Telekinesis: What is it?*

I positioned my pen on the notebook and opened up the *Telekinesis For Beginners* book to begin my research. The image on the first page nearly took my breath away. The realistic illustration showed a profile of a human head, and at the center of the forehead was a glowing yellow eye. My hand wrapped around the purple gel pen as I fixed my gaze on that eye. My own forehead began to tingle as I released my grip on the gel pen. Looking into that yellow eye filled me with fear and a sense of something else that I hadn't experienced before; I felt almost powerful. I couldn't look away. A low buzz hummed in my ear, and I realized that I was no longer holding the pen, yet from the corner of my eye, I could tell that it was still erect, balanced on its tip.

"Tiffany?"

I blinked and the humming in my ears stopped. The pen fell to the table as I glanced up from the book. Judy stared down at me, her forehead scrunched in concern.

"I didn't know you were still back here, sweetie. I thought you left!" She gasped and held her hand to her chest. "Child, your mother called, looking for you! She says you were supposed to meet her at the food court."

"What time is it?" I flicked my wrist. The alarm I had set to remind me to meet Momma had gone off. It was already 2:12 P.M. "Oh my gosh."

"Be sure to put those books away," Judy said.

"I will." I turned off the alarm and stood, disoriented. I must have fallen asleep. I packed up my gym bag and brought the books back to the New Age/Occult shelf, still in a daze. I waved to Judy and fast-walked out of the store and into the now-busy mall, my heart racing. I had gone to the bookstore for answers, but I left with even more questions than before.

Chapter Three

T elekinesis is a fun word to say, isn't it? Sounds a little like telephone. Anyway, the rest of the afternoon, all I could think about was what I read in that book about telekinesis. I dunno if I could really move things with my mind. Maybe that was what was going on with me. Maybe I was really a witch, and I would get a magical amulet on my 16th birthday like in my favorite movie Teen Witch. Maybe it was all in my head.

"Everything okay, baby? Is there anything else you need?" Momma gave me a funny sort of look as she leaned over and kissed me on the cheek later that day.

"I'm fine," I lied.

"Mmm," she said, her lips all screwed up into a sort of half smile, half frown. "You just seem kind of off to me. I don't know... something's different."

"Just worried about the pageant is all," I shrugged. The last thing I wanted to do was make Momma worry. "I'm fine really."

I balanced a to-go box of salad on my lap later that afternoon. I was already making Momma late, and she needed to get back to work before her lunch break was over. For the first time, I really and truly didn't want to go to dance class. There was a pit in my stomach that just clawed and clawed at me, and the thought of Miss Suzy yelling all night made me want to puke. But I knew how hard Momma worked so that I could dance and compete, so I didn't want to make trouble. Still, the concerned look on her face told me that I wasn't foolin' anyone.

"Something's up," Momma said. "Spill it."

"I don't think I want to compete in pageants anymore."

"Why not?" Momma tilted her head. "I know you might be getting a little old for the kiddie pageants, but I figured we could start looking into pre-teen pageants if you wanted."

I shrugged. "It's not fun anymore."

"Are the girls being mean?"

"No." I pursed my lips. "Miss Suzy is acting real mean though."

"I know she can be tough sometimes. Plus, I think that the studio isn't doing so well financially. It's hard to run a business."

"Yeah, but she's never been mean like this before."

"Well, tell ya what," Momma said. "Finish up this last pageant. We already paid the entry fee and you've already put so much work in. Then after Christmas we can take a break and you can figure out what you want to do next. Does that sound like a deal?"

I smiled and nodded. "Deal."

"Good girl." Momma leaned over and gave me another kiss. "I'll be back at eight on the nose. I won't be late tonight."

"Promise?" I held out my pinky finger.

Momma looped her pinky around mine and shook. "Promise."

"Tell Tony thanks for the big salad," I said, opening the door. "I love you."

"Love you too, Punkin'."

I stepped out of Momma's car and onto the sidewalk in front of Suzy Dawn Dance Studio, with my guts all tied up in knots. I definitely didn't want to be there, but I knew that I had to. Momma taught me that it was important to finish the things that we started, and not to waste money. Quitting was not an option, and even though I hated the way that I was feeling, there was a silver lining. If Momma said that I could quit after this last pageant, then I knew she meant it. As I walked through the doors of the dance studio, I felt relieved and a little sad to know that it would be my last time.

I slipped into the waiting room and settled in on a bench where I would wait until my class started at 5:00 P.M. Like everywhere else, the waiting room at the dance studio was decorated for the holidays with cartoon reindeer, Santas, and a big Christmas tree with a bunch of presents underneath. The presents weren't real; they were just empty boxes wrapped to look like presents, but I still liked to pretend that there were gifts for us all inside. I spent a lot of time in that waiting room over the years and usually kept myself busy reading or talking to the parents that were waiting for their kids to get out of private lessons with Miss Suzy. There was no one else in the waiting room but I didn't mind; I had my salad and my notes from the bookstore to keep me busy until class started, so the waiting part wasn't so bad. It felt safer to be alone inside rather than outside, staring at the woods beyond the parking lot, anyway.

I took off my faux fur coat, opened up my to-go box, and dug into my big salad, enjoying every ranch-dressing-drenched bite of cucumber, tomato, and carrots. When my salad was finished, I tucked the to-go box in my gym bag and pulled out my Trapper Keeper. I had written down a bunch of notes from the bookstore, but I also wanted to write down everything that had happened so far. I got out my gel pen and got to work.

Tiffany Baldwin

December 16, 1993

Dear Diary,

Last night something weird happened…

I wrote and wrote until my hand got tired. I wrote down everything from the exploding parking lot light to my headaches and the weird glowing eyes. Before I knew it, nearly an hour had passed, and more girls began to file into the waiting room. First came Jennifer. She was my age, but we didn't talk much, even though we had been in the same dance class since kindergarten. Jennifer was really pretty and had long dark hair that she wore on top of her head in a bun. She was also really, really skinny. I overheard Momma mumble to herself once that she was worried about how thin she was getting. Then a few other girls came in, each of them familiar to me but not necessarily friendly. We all sat quietly and watched the clock over the door until it was our turn to go into the studio. I kept glancing toward the door, wondering when Samantha would come to class. She was my only real friend at Suzy Dawn Dance Studio.

Finally, five minutes before class, Samantha and her grandma hurried through the front door. Samantha's hair hung down in her face and her grandma smelled of cigarettes as they sat next to me. My salad churned in my stomach as Samantha's grandmother yanked her hair into a braid, grumbling about how she was going to be late for Bingo. I was relieved when she finally left, but my insides still felt like a swarm of bees.

"Hi." I gave Samantha a forced smile.

She didn't smile back. "Hi."

"You okay?"

"No." Samantha sighed. "Grandma is having a bad day again."

"I'm sorry." I felt bad. She looked so small and defeated and I didn't have a snack or a juice box or anything to offer her this time. "Do you need a hug?"

Samantha nodded.

I wrapped my arm around her shoulders and squeezed her. "It's gonna be okay."

"There's something I wanted to ask you," Samantha said, staring up at me. "Did you see the —"

The dance studio door burst open, and a red-faced teenage girl stormed through the waiting room. Everyone in the room audibly gasped as she flew out the door in a flurry of tulle and tears. This wasn't the first time I had seen the teen crying as she left one of Miss Suzy's private tutoring lessons. When I was younger, I thought that I wanted to do *en pointe* ballet, but after seeing so many of the teenage girls come out of class crying over bloody feet and rolled ankles, I changed my mind.

"Was that Paulina?" Jennifer whispered to me.

I nodded. "I think so."

"I heard she had a broken toe," she said. "Miss Suzy is making her dance this weekend, anyway."

"That sucks."

I clenched my teeth as Miss Suzy appeared in the doorway. Her face was pinched as she gazed out into the waiting room at her students. She clapped her hands and all of us stood at attention.

"Come, girls. Miss Tonya is waiting."

"Everybody warmed up? Yes? Alright, let's get into position then!" Miss Tonya stood at the front of the dance studio, all smiles and toned, athletic limbs. She adjusted the scrunchie on top of her head, her tight midriff just briefly exposed as she raised her arms. I took my place in line and my chest flooded with warmth as I admired her new pink spandex bike shorts and neon green crop top ensemble. Miss Tonya was the assistant dance instructor, and she looked just like Christina Applegate and I loved her. Before she worked for Miss Suzy, Miss Tonya was one of her students and was even a runner-up in the 1989 Florida Miss Teen Pageant. She was only a few years older than us girls and felt more like a big sister than our dance teacher.

"You girls are gonna love the music for today," Miss Tonya said. "This is Ace of Base."

Miss Tonya pressed play and an electronic beat buzzed through my body. The thudding bass line pulsed from the soles of my feet all the way up and the hairs on the back of my neck stood on end as the music flowed through me. I loved music almost as much as I loved to dance. Moving along to the big, booming stereo system was probably my favorite part of being at Suzy Dawn Dance Studio. When Miss Suzy or Miss Tonya played high-energy electronic music, I didn't just hear it, I *felt* it. No matter how tired I was, if they put that music on, my body just wanted to move. It was almost as if the thumping music recharged my batteries or something.

"And stretch, and lean, and one, two, three!"

We mirrored Miss Tonya's moves as the woman sang about all the things that she wanted. I didn't understand what she meant, but the singer had a nice voice, and the lyrics were catchy. By the end of the song, my bangs were stuck to my forehead and temples in sweaty clumps, and I was breathing hard. We danced through two more songs and then another one came on about some lady who saw a sign. After that song, Miss Tonya let us rest and get a water break. This was just our warm-up for the first day of rehearsal run-through, but it was the part of class that I liked the most. I took my usual spot on the floor and smiled as Samantha joined me on the sidelines. Her little features were serious, her lips set in a thin, tight line.

"Did you see the eyes last night?" She took a sip from her water bottle and blinked at me.

My legs went numb and tingly. "What eyes?"

"The glowing eyes in the woods. I saw them last night after practice. Did you see them too?"

"I think I did," I said, my eyebrows scrunched together. "I thought maybe I imagined it."

I frowned, not knowing what to say next. The eyes, my headaches, the busted parking lot light. So many weird things were happening all at once that bothered me. But more than anything, I was worried about Samantha.

"Samantha?" I asked.

"What?"

"Who drove you home last night?"

"My uncle," she said.

"He sounded mean, too."

"He is."

"Are you okay?" I asked.

Samantha shrugged. "I guess. I can't stop thinking about those eyes, though."

"What do you think the eyes belonged to?" I sipped on my water, staring around the room. "A stray cat or something?"

"I don't think so."

"Did you ever see them before?" I asked.

Samantha gazed at me with big eyes. "I dunno. I see them sometimes when I get angry or sad."

"Have you ever told your grandma or anyone about it?"

She shook her head. "Grown-ups wouldn't believe me."

"You're probably right," I said. "Well, I believe you. I saw them, but I wasn't sure until just now."

"You have to be careful though," Samantha said, her voice a whisper. "Don't look at them too long or—"

"Okay girls, time to start the run-through!" Miss Suzy burst onto the studio floor. She had changed out of her black ballet instructor ensemble into her favorite floral leotard and white tights, so I could tell she meant business. Samantha and I snapped to attention, stood up, and took our place in line. We knew better than to lag behind on a pageant run-through day.

"We need to get this show down to a tight three hours!" Miss Suzy turned to the stereo. "That means you need to have a parent backstage with you to help you with your hair, makeup, and costume changes. Does everyone have a parent that will be with them this Saturday?"

"*Yes, Miss Suzy.*" We all chimed in unison.

"Good. Okay, it's 5 P.M. now. I'm going to take five minutes at the beginning to introduce you all and talk about the dance school, then it's show time. Let's begin!"

I nodded, readying myself for the long night ahead. I had done pageant run-throughs tons of times before, so I knew what to expect. Practices were long and tedious, and everyone had to sit quietly and still as we waited for our turn. We had one more full run-through practice tomorrow at the venue downtown before showtime on Saturday morning.

We performed the group tap routine flawlessly and took our spots on the sidelines. Miss Tonya was the opening act, performing a high-energy dance routine to *Pump Up the Volume*. After that, it was Jennifer who did a solo ballet dance to *The Nutcracker Suite*, and then Samantha with her baton routine. I clapped the loudest when Samantha finished because she did such a good job, and I knew she needed the encouragement. The night ticked on, and a dozen other girls went up showing off their talents; Kyra played *Silent Night* on an electric piano, and another pretty little girl sang *Somewhere Over the Rainbow*. My heart sank a little because she was a much better singer than me, and she was younger and cuter, but I smiled and clapped for her, anyway.

Finally, it was my turn to go up and sing. I grabbed my cassette tape from my gym bag and walked across the studio floor, my tap shoes clacking as I handed the tape to Miss Tonya. She smiled at me and patted me on the back and told me 'good luck'. I held my breath because I definitely did need good luck for what I was about to do next. I glanced over at Miss Suzy to see if she was paying attention, but she was only filing her nails and looked disinterested. This was probably going to be my last pageant, so I wanted to take a chance. I wanted to do my routine my way.

The beginning chords for *Jingle Bell Rock* flowed through the studio and my already racing heart picked up speed. I launched into the spirited tap routine that I had been practicing in secret and belted out the lyrics to my favorite Christmas song. At home, wearing my homemade Christmas tree suit, the routine was perfect, and I knew that if I could just show Miss Suzy how it looked for the talent portion she would approve. But as I launched into the second chorus, the music stopped, and I was left singing to thin air.

"Tiffany, what is this?" Miss Suzy held up the cassette, its tape guts hanging down in sad brown ribbons. Her face was red, and her eyes were bugged open wide as she shook the cassette at me.

"You broke my tape!"

"You're wasting our time," she said, tossing the tape into a nearby trash can. "Go sit back down."

"But, Miss Suzy..."

"No! You're going to perform the agreed-upon routine on Saturday, and that's *final*."

"I never agreed to anything," I grumbled.

"Tiffany, take your seat!"

I glanced around the room as the crowd of girls stared back at me. I was expecting them to laugh at me or be mad or embarrassed at the very least. As my gaze zeroed in on Samantha, she and all of the other girls didn't look angry or annoyed; they just looked *sad*. I blinked as fresh tears spilled down my hot cheeks, my tap shoes making loud clackety noises that only seemed to punctuate my shame. So much for putting myself out there.

I sat back down and tried really hard not to cry, but I couldn't help it. The tears began to flow as Lacy took the floor and began her ballet routine for *Greensleeves*. I didn't get it. Why was Miss Suzy being so mean to me? My routine was no different from the other girls. Why wouldn't she just let me do what I wanted? I sat there seething as a dark cloud invaded my mind. I tried to hold in the tears and the harder I tried, the more my head began to hurt. Just like before, the pain focused in the center of my head, right between my eyes, throbbing, dull, and achy. The more I thought about how unfair Miss Suzy was being, the angrier I got. I watched Lacy's routine through a headache and tears until she spun, tripped, and fell.

Lacy laid in a heap on the dance floor. Sparkles of adrenaline rushed through my veins as she pushed up onto her hands and stared into the mirror with a stunned expression on her face. She met my gaze and broke into a sob. Just like me and Samantha, she seemed to be at her breaking point. Lacy hung her head and wailed.

The center of my forehead began to buzz again. I glanced at my reflection in the mirror again and for a moment, I swore my eyes were on fire.

"Get up, Lacy!" Miss Suzy shouted. "We don't have time for —"
THWACK.

A chorus of screams pierced through the studio as a crack etched down the center of the mirrored panel along the back wall. The jagged split cut down the middle of the mirror like a bolt of lightning, creeping down to create a spiderweb reflection of fragmented faces. Miss Suzy barely had time to move before a large, splintered piece fell away and shattered at her feet.

Chapter Four

"**A**nd then, there were a million little pieces of mirror everywhere!"

Momma stared at me, confused, as I slid into the passenger seat later that night. Class ran a little longer than usual because Miss Suzy and Miss Tonya took so long to clean up the broken mirror. I was glad in a way though, that practice ran late. Momma had already been waiting for me in her car and I didn't have to worry about being alone in the dark. The parking lot light was still broken, and I was too scared to stare out into the woods and catch a glimpse of the creepy eyes again.

"That sounds so dangerous," Momma said, throwing the car into drive. "Did someone throw something at the mirror?"

"No. It just broke."

"Well, thank goodness no one got hurt," Momma said. "Those mirrors are expensive. I bet Miss Suzy was upset."

"No more upset than usual," I said. "She also threw my cassette tape in the trash."

"Which one?"

"Jingle Bell Rock."

"I thought you weren't going to do that for the talent portion?"

I shrugged. "I figured maybe if Miss Suzy saw how good it was, she would change her mind."

"Why did she throw the cassette away?"

"I dunno. She was mad, and the tape unraveled," I said. "I told you, she seems to just be getting meaner and meaner. I really don't want to go back to class after the pageant."

"You don't have to," Momma said, pursing her lips. "I'm going to have a nice long chat with Suzanne, though."

Suzanne. A flood of love and pride washed over me as I glanced at my mom. She only said people's full names like that when she was mad. If I knew my Momma, Miss Suzy was going to get an earful for throwing out my cassette tape.

Momma tossed her head back and let out a long, slow breath. "What time do we need to be at the Civic Center tomorrow?"

"The first run through is from 9:00 A.M. until noon. Then we break for lunch and have a dress rehearsal from 2:00 P.M. to 5:00 P.M."

"Shoot. Why did they have to plan this thing the weekend before Christmas? I'm going to burn up so much gas driving back and forth from work tomorrow."

"I'm sorry, Momma."

"It's not your fault. I wish I could have asked for time off, but it's just too darn busy before the holidays. We'll just have to get to bed early tonight so I can do your hair before I drop you off," Momma said. "Do you still have that Pizza Hut certificate?"

"Yeah."

"We can go get your personal pan pizza after I get off work if you want."

"Isn't Pizza Hut too expensive?" I asked.

"It's a special occasion," Momma said. "Besides, I have a coupon for the salad bar. You read all those books. You don't want that certificate to go to waste, do you?"

"No."

"It's settled then." She gave me a concerned sideways glance. "What's the matter, Tiff? I thought you would be excited?"

"I am," I paused. "It's just... Momma, something isn't right."

"What do you mean?"

"I don't know how to explain it," I said. "Miss Suzy is so mean to all the girls these days, not just me. I don't think anyone at Suzy Dawn has fun anymore."

"Why? Did something else happen?"

"I don't know! Things just seem so strange." I sucked in a deep breath. "Also, there's this little girl, Samantha. Her family isn't very nice to her. I'm worried about her."

"She's the one who lives with her grandma?"

"Yeah."

"Poor little thing." Momma grew quiet and kept her eyes on the road.

Now and then, I asked Momma where my Grandma was. Growing up, I didn't think much about the fact that it was just us two; it seemed normal for my family to only be me and Momma. But as I got older, I realized that other kids had cousins and aunts and uncles and grandparents. We didn't have anybody. Momma said it was because her family up north wasn't very nice to her. When it came to asking about my dad, I knew not to bring him up, either. It only made her cry.

All the rest of the ride home, I couldn't stop thinking about the shattered mirror and Jennifer and Samantha and even pretty Paulina, the *en pointe* ballerina. Miss Suzy had always been a little bit strict when she was teaching class, but never this bad. Suzy Dawn Dance Studio used to be like a second home for me; a place where I felt safe and surrounded by people that loved the same things I did. Now, everything felt off, and all I wanted to do was run away.

When we got home from the dance studio, Momma reheated the cheeseburgers from the night before while I took a quick shower. We got out the TV trays and watched some old black-and-white Christmas movies as we ate dinner. My stomach was all scrunched up in knots, but I shoved the cheeseburger down, anyway. Like usual, Momma didn't last through the whole movie and was knocked out cold before 10 P.M. I turned down the volume and padded toward the TV cart where my VHS collection was and pulled out a mixtape of my favorite shows. I spent all summer break learning how to record reruns on dozens of tapes. This one had six hours of my favorites, including *90210, Saved by the Bell, Clarissa Explains it All* and *Are You Afraid of the Dark?* I cuddled up next to Momma on the couch and fell asleep to the comforting glow of the TV.

"Good luck today, baby! I'll see you after practice!"

"Bye, Momma!"

I stepped out on the sidewalk, waved, and closed the passenger door of her car the following morning. I had to be careful getting out of the car; Momma had piled all my hair up on top of my head in a big curly bun and set my bangs into a perfect arc with about a half a can of hairspray. I could still taste the White Rain extra-hold formula hairspray on my tongue as I slung my bag over my shoulder and glanced up at the front of the civic center. I turned to watch her car drive away and a sick sort of feeling entered my gut. I was all alone and Momma wouldn't be back to get me for a long time. I gritted my teeth and threw my shoulders back as I walked toward the entrance of the building. I had to be a big girl and take care of myself, just for today.

The auditorium at the civic center was dark and empty when I wandered in, and a creepy sensation edged up my spine. I breathed in the musty air conditioning and tossed my gym bag onto the nearest folding seat, half scared and half happy to be all alone. I didn't mind having to come in early, but I did feel funny being the only one there. Still, I had everything I needed for the day. I had my breakfast (a bagel and grapes), my lunch (a cold McDonald's cheeseburger and an apple), and a bunch of juice boxes. It was going to be a long, grueling day of practicing and waiting, but I brought my Trapper Keeper and a few books to keep me busy until it was my turn to perform. I cracked open a dog-eared paperback of *The Baby-Sitter's Club* and was just about to settle in when Miss Suzy stomped onto the stage.

"We need draped layers of gold garland here. Did you get the curtain of white lights?"

I scooted my body down as far as I could go into the seat and watched as Miss Suzy and a man with a mustache walked to the center of the stage. The man was wearing a pair of coveralls that made him look like a janitor or something. He scratched the back of his neck, sighed, and gave her an annoyed look. I held my breath as they talked, trying not to make a sound.

"Yeah, we got 'em," the man said. "I got some bad news about the spotlights, though. The wiring is shoddy, and my boss said we can't get them replaced until after the new year."

"So?" Miss Suzy crossed her arms at her chest and squared up to him.

"So, they're not safe to use," the man said. "I don't know what to tell you."

"We can't have a pageant of lights without lights!" Miss Suzy shouted. "It's too late to change the venue. Can't you just wrap some electrical tape around the wires or something?"

"I guess," the guy sighed. "It ain't safe, though."

"Good."

My chest hurt as I continued to hold my breath. I scrunched even further into the seat to try to make myself invisible, but forgot about the book in my lap. The paperback fell to the floor in a flutter of pages and made a loud sound that smacked through the empty auditorium. Miss Suzy and the man turned their attention to me, and I gasped.

"Who's there?" Miss Suzy shielded her eyes. "Tiffany? Is that you?"

"Hi, Miss Suzy."

"You're early," she said.

I cleared my throat. "Yep. Just waiting for rehearsal."

"Good. You can make yourself useful then." She walked backstage and returned with a big cardboard box. She hauled the box down the stage side stairs as the man in coveralls walked to the back of the stage and began working with a giant spool of silver garland.

"Here." Miss Suzy placed the box at my feet. "These are the programs. I need you to fold them all neatly in half and place them back in the box. You can get the other girls to help you while you wait."

"Uh, okay." I bit my lip and gave the box a skeptical glance. There must have been a thousand pages in the box to fold.

"Thank you." Miss Suzy turned on her heels and fast-walked back up to the stage, pumping her arms at her side. She let out a loud, audible groan as she marched back toward the man hanging the garland.

"I said gold garland! Not silver!"

I picked up one of the programs and began to read.

Suzy Dawn Dance Studio Presents

The 13th Annual

PAGEANT OF LIGHTS

Saturday, December 18, 1993

I flipped to the back of the program, where all the names were. Two dozen girls would be going on before me. Finally, I found my name. Tiffany Baldwin, Age 9, Singing *Have Yourself a Merry Little Christmas*

I frowned and folded the program in half. I wished that it said *Jingle Bell Rock* instead, but there was nothing I could do about that now. If this was going to be my last performance, then I needed to chin up and make the best of it. I grabbed another paper and folded it, then another and another. I folded faster and faster, creating a pile of paper names and songs and dances, hopes and dreams. One of the girls in that program was going to win the Pageant of Lights, but I knew deep down that it wasn't going to be me. I folded again and again, zipping through the job faster and faster until a sharp pain sliced through my forefinger.

The headache returned as I stared down at my hand, the pain more intense and throbbing than ever. A kaleidoscope of color flashed before my eyes as I gasped and held out my hand in the low light. A thin bloom of red pulsed from a paper cut on the pad of my pointer finger. I stuck my finger in my mouth and sucked at the penny-flavored blood until the dull pain in my forehead subsided.

Chapter Five

"I like your hair."

Jennifer slumped down in a chair next to me later that morning as all the other girls began to file into the auditorium. I picked at the bandage on my index finger and glanced up at her, not sure if she was being nice or mean. Even though we had been in dance class together for years and had competed against each other in dozens of pageants, Jennifer never really talked to me before. I eyed her skeptically and wondered why she chose that moment to talk to me.

"Thanks." I put down the last folded pamphlet. It took me an hour, but I managed to finish the entire box myself. It turned out that there weren't a thousand papers to fold, but there might as well have been.

"Is it permed?"

"No," I self-consciously reached a hand to my sprayed bangs. They hadn't moved an inch and were still perfectly arced in a wave.

"I wanted to get my hair permed, but my stepmom won't let me," Jennifer said, hugging her knees to her chest.

"I heard the chemicals ruin your hair anyway," I said. "Do you need something?"

"Miss Suzy asked me to come see if you need any help folding the programs."

"No. I'm all done," I said. "Thanks anyway."

Jennifer pulled out her water bottle and a baggie of rice cakes from her gym bag. She nibbled on one of the rice cakes and sat next to me quietly as we watched the rest of the students from Suzy Dawn Dance Studio settle into their seats. Most of the girls that were there had their mother or an adult with them to help with costume changes and hair and makeup touch-ups. Jennifer and I were the only ones without an adult around.

"I liked your routine," Jennifer finally said, putting her unfinished rice cake away. "The *Jingle Bell Rock* one. I wish Miss Suzy would have let you do it."

"Really?" My shoulders relaxed. I offered her a weak smile and pulled out my breakfast. "Thanks."

I opened up the packet of cream cheese and began to slather my bagel. Bagels were okay on their own, but cream cheese was my true love. The more the better. I glanced over at Jennifer as she stared at my breakfast with an open mouth.

"What?"

"Nothing." She sighed and dug into her bag of rice cakes. "I just wish I could have a bagel."

"You wanna share mine?" I held out half of my breakfast to her.

Jennifer paused and stared down at the cream-cheese-covered bagel half. "I can't. I'm not supposed to."

"Why not?"

"My stepmom says I shouldn't. Plus, Miss Suzy says I can't eat that stuff if I want to do *en pointe* ballet someday."

"Oh." I glanced down at her lap. We were the same age, but her thighs were half the size of mine. "Jennifer?"

"Yeah?"

"Does competing in pageants make you happy?"

Jennifer shrugged. "It used to."

"I think this is going to be my last one," I said. "I love to dance, but I don't like how competing makes me feel anymore."

"I wish I could quit," she said, yawning. "I'm so tired and hungry all the time. Everything hurts and Miss Suzy is so mean."

"Why can't you quit?"

Jennifer shrugged. "I don't think I can."

"Did you tell your stepmom any of this?"

"No."

"Attention everyone!"

Jennifer and I snapped into pageant-ready mode and turned our faces toward the front of the auditorium. Miss Suzy stood front and center, dressed in an oversized reindeer sweater and a pair of red and white striped candy cane leggings. She had applied heavy stage makeup, and her hair was teased out in a big fan around her face, her blue shadow-lidded eyes determined and focused as a shark behind a curtain of thick black lashes.

"Thank you all so much for being here on time and ready to go. We have a lot of work to do today, but I know we can get through these rehearsals without a hitch! Parents, please pay attention to the time and make sure your child is prepared for their turn on stage. Let's make this a great Pageant of Lights!"

Miss Suzy clapped, her applause echoing through the auditorium.

The audience took a moment to clap back with what seemed like forced enthusiasm. I slipped out of my sneakers and into my tap shoes and headed toward the stage for the group dance number. I had performed at the Civic Center dozens of times and knew my way backstage. I used to get butterflies of excitement when I would climb the stairs to the shiny wooden stage. I used to love the way that the heavy red velvet curtains felt against my skin as I brushed past them, the sound of my heels clacking against the polished floor. I even loved the bright stage lights that made it hard for me to see. This time, I didn't feel excited. I only felt dread.

Miss Suzy and Miss Tonya guided us to our marks, placing Samantha front and center, with me in the back and all of the other girls in between. My heartbeat *glug, glug, glugged* in my ears as I watched all the dancers take their places. Something felt wrong, and I didn't know what it was. I glanced up at the stage lights and blinked as one of the bulbs flickered.

The wiring is shoddy.

The words of the Civic Center maintenance man rang in my ears as the opening notes of *Gonna Make You Sweat* boomed through the auditorium. I pushed my anxiety down and focused, staring out straight into the empty rows of seats as we launched into the dance. Thirty girls tapped, shuffled, smiled, and posed in sync with one another while the light overhead flickered. I stared at the back of Samantha's tightly braided head as the song began to wind down, then back up at the flickering light again.

Move.

A low sort of whine drowned out the music as a voice I had never heard before whispered in my ear. I lowered my arms and stopped dancing as the other girls continued to tap around me. I glanced up at the flickering stage light and, I dunno, my instincts took over. At that very moment, I knew that something bad was about to happen, and the image of Samantha crushed beneath the weight of the fallen light flashed before my eyes.

Do it. Do it now.

I pushed the girls in front of me out of the way and hurled my body toward Samantha. My chest was tight, and my limbs were heavy, almost as if I were underwater and couldn't breathe. Still, I forced myself to move and grabbed Samantha by the shoulders. I pulled her back, even as Miss Suzy screamed at me from the front row. I kept moving Samantha to safety and the other girls moved out of the way too, just in time for the stage light to come crashing down right on her mark.

After the stage light fell, practice for the pageant came to a halt. Girls ran from the stage, screaming and falling into their parents' open arms. I watched as a few adults exchanged harsh words with Miss Suzy. Our pageant director painted on an apologetic, appalled expression as she tried to assure the panicked parents that everything would be okay. A few parents walked out, but most of us stayed put and waited as maintenance swept up the debris from the fallen light. The mood in the auditorium was chaotic and frenzied, and more than ever, I didn't feel safe to be there.

Miss Suzy yelled at the maintenance man and continued to placate parents as I sat back in my seat, alone. I didn't know what it felt like to be in shock, but I thought that maybe I was in it. I could still sense the tremor of the heavy light in my body as it crashed to the floor, feel the scratchy material of Samantha's costume on my forearms as I dragged her away. I don't know what it was that told me to grab her and move her out of the way, but I was grateful for it. The thought of Samantha's crushed little body buried beneath the fallen light burned into my brain and was an image that would not leave.

During the chaos, Samantha kept giving me strange looks from her spot seated next to her grandmother. For a moment, I was a little jealous as she leaned against her grandmother's shoulder and wiped at her tear-stained cheeks. Even though her grandma was mean sometimes, at least Samantha had someone to be there with her. I was still so scared from the light falling and no one had come to check up on me. Not until Miss Tonya came over to see me later that morning, anyway.

"Hey, sweetie. You want me to call your Momma?" Miss Tonya pushed the folding auditorium seat down and sat next to me as I hugged myself in my chair. I stared up at the stage, now slightly less bright due to the single missing stage light. I glanced back up at Miss Tonya and tried my best not to look upset.

"It's okay. She has to work. I don't want to bother her."

"Are you sure? I bet you were awfully scared. I know I was."

"I'll be alright." I pushed my bangs from my eyes. I certainly *wasn't* alright, but I didn't want Miss Tonya to know that. "Is Miss Suzy mad?"

"About what?"

"That I made us stop practice."

"It wasn't your fault at all." Miss Tonya placed a hand on my shoulder. "Tiffany, you're a *hero*. That little girl would have been hurt very badly or worse if you didn't move her out of the way."

"I guess." I stared at my lap. "Are we still going to have practice?"

"As soon as they clean up the stage." Miss Tonya nodded and gave me a funny kind of sideways look. "How did you know the light was going to fall, anyway?"

"I heard the maintenance guy say that the wiring wasn't safe."

"You did?"

"Mhmm. Before everyone got here, he tried to tell Miss Suzy. She wouldn't listen."

"Hmm." Miss Tonya removed her hand from my shoulder, crossed her arms under her chest, and let out a long huff of breath. "Figures."

"What?"

"Miss Suzy's got a lot of money riding on this pageant." Miss Tonya pursed her lips. "I can't believe she would ..."

My eyes grew wide as Miss Tonya turned her attention back to me. She unfolded her arms and softened her expression.

"Sorry, I shouldn't have said anything. I just wanted to come over and make sure you were doing okay."

"I'm fine."

Miss Tonya smiled and nodded. "Come see me if you need anything?"

"I will."

"Okay, I gotta get back. I'm up next once the stage is cleared."

"Be careful." The words came out of my mouth somber and insistent, but I meant them. I loved Miss Tonya, and out of all the adults, she was one of the only ones who really cared about us. I didn't want to see her get hurt, too.

"It'll be okay, Tiffany." She smiled. "Promise."

Chapter Six

The atmosphere felt off the rest of the day during pageant practice. Miss Tonya's dance routine got off to a shaky start, but by the end of *Pump Up the Volume*, she seemed to have found her rhythm again. My fondness for Miss Tonya only grew as I watched her perform, all smiles and joy, as she danced a routine that she had choreographed herself. Miss Tonya's arms and legs were so strong and toned, and like me, she wasn't exactly a toothpick. Seeing Miss Tonya having fun on stage made me think that maybe there was still a place for me in the dance world after all.

Everyone was a little quieter than usual and kept to themselves in the aftermath of the broken stage light. I usually read while I waited for my turn to perform during pageant practices, but this time, I couldn't concentrate on the book I brought. Since I wasn't allowed to do the routine that I wanted, all my excitement for the pageant was gone. When it was my turn to go up and sing, I felt like a robot. I wasn't in the mood to have a merry little Christmas anymore, and it didn't matter anyway since Miss Suzy didn't seem to care.

Jennifer's ballet routine for *The Nutcracker Suite* was probably my favorite. I always loved the classic Christmas ballet and, even though I wasn't much in the spirit, I still enjoyed the music and the dance. Miss Suzy watched her from the edge of the stage like a hawk and only had to remind her to point her toe and hold her hands up once. Up on stage under the bright lights, the dark circles under Jennifer's eyes really stood out, and she would have to cover it up with some heavy pancake makeup for the pageant. She was clearly becoming Miss Suzy's new favorite student, and it made sense. Jennifer fit the mold of what Miss Suzy thought a dancer should look and act like.

As practice droned on, it seemed like Miss Suzy lost interest in the other girls' routines, too. Kyra messed up a few times on her piano, and Samantha seemed completely lost up on stage with her little baton. The only other time Miss Suzy stood at the edge of the stage to watch and offer critique was during Paulina's *en pointe* routine. Paulina was performing a dance from *The Sleeping Beauty*, and like Jennifer, she sure seemed sleepy.

Paulina's routine started out flawlessly, just as always. Her back and legs were straight, and she hit all of her marks. After her first big jump, though, something changed. Her placid, focused expression broke, and she winced as she rose up on her right toe. Paulina twirled once, twice, three times. Blooms of red began to mar the outside of her battered pink satin practice slippers, and by the time the song was over, it looked like Paulina could barely keep herself upright. She completed her routine with tears in her eyes.

"Well done, Paulina," Miss Suzy said. "Wrap that toe better for the dress rehearsal."

Paulina pursed her lips together in a tight line and propped her hands on her hips. She nodded, teary-eyed, and walked off the stage.

Miss Suzy stepped center stage and glanced up at the lights. She grabbed a microphone and addressed the audience.

"I want to thank everyone who stuck around after the incident with the broken stage light. Rest assured, I've spoken with maintenance and all the other equipment is safe and secure so the show can go on." Miss Suzy met my gaze and cleared her throat. "We're going to break for lunch now and skip the interview portion of rehearsal since we had a delay. Be back here and ready for a full dress rehearsal at 2 P.M."

The crowd murmured, and everyone rose from their seats as Miss Suzy took off toward backstage. I stayed frozen in my seat, anxious that Miss Suzy would come find me and scold me for causing the light to drop from the sky somehow. I pulled out my book and my lunch and tried to relax, but all I wanted to do was go home. I thought about calling Momma and letting her know what happened, but I knew that I needed to let her work. I wanted to tell her what I was feeling and seeing and hearing, but it was like little Samantha said; grown-ups wouldn't believe us, anyway.

The full pageant dress rehearsal went smoother than the first run through, and as promised, we were finished by 5 P.M. I was so tired by the time Momma came to pick me up, I nearly forgot about going out for pizza afterwards. I watched all the other girls leave with their parents, lugging garment bags of sparkling costumes and suitcases full of makeup and curling irons and medical tape. I was still wearing the green velvet dress Momma had gotten for me for the interview portion of the pageant when she came to pick me up. I probably wouldn't get many other chances to wear it, so I wanted to get as much mileage out of the pretty special occasion dress as I could.

At a quarter after five, Momma's Toyota pulled into the Civic Center parking lot. Unlike the dance studio, the Civic Center was smack dab in the middle of downtown, and there were no thick woods where flashing eyes could hide. Still, I felt uneasy as I waited and moved faster than usual when Momma pulled up to the curb. I grabbed my bags and slid into the passenger seat, happy to be one step closer to never seeing Suzy Dawn Dance Studio or a pageant stage again. Momma looked tired and gave me what I knew was her forced smile as WINK 96.9 played Christmas music on the radio.

"How did it go?"

"Alright," I said, clicking my seatbelt. "There was an accident, though."

"An accident? What kind?"

"A stage light fell. Almost crashed into Samantha. I pulled her out of the way in time."

"What! Is everyone okay?"

"Yeah. We were all a little spooked, but you know how Miss Suzy is. *The show must go on.*"

"Oh, Tiffany." Momma's voice wavered. "I should have been there with you today."

I glanced over at Momma as she threw the car into drive. Her eyes shone with tears, and I wished that I had never told her about the accident or about wanting to quit pageants or any of it.

"It's okay. I know you had to work. You'll be with me tomorrow."

Momma sniffed and glanced over at me. "Still feel like getting pizza?"

I nodded. "I *always* feel like getting pizza."

"Good girl."

The sun was setting as we arrived at the Pizza Hut near our apartment complex, and I let go of my worries just enough to allow myself to get excited again. I got out of the car, shrugged into my faux fur coat, and dug my free personal pan pizza coupon from my bag. The December air was crisp, the restaurant was brightly decorated for the season, and I felt like a superstar strolling across the Pizza Hut threshold with my hard-earned coupon at hand.

We found a booth by the window, and Momma ordered a pitcher of soda from our server. I slid my pizza coupon across the table and ordered a personal pan pizza with mushrooms and black olives. Momma ordered the salad bar, and we eased into our seats, enjoying the restaurant ambience. I stared across the table at my momma, exhausted and anticipating our meal. For a moment, all was right with the world.

"It's been a long time since we ate at Pizza Hut," Momma said, folding her hands on top of the table. "This is nice."

"Not since my birthday."

"Mhmm." Momma yawned. "I wish I could take you out to dinner every night."

The server brought us our pitcher of soda. I poured a generous amount into the red plastic cup filled with ice. Momma stared out the window, as though she were in a daze.

"Momma? Everything okay?"

"Oh." She gasped and sucked in a breath. "Yeah, fine. Everything's fine. A customer was rude to me today, and it's that time of the month, so I'm just feeling a little delicate."

"That time of the month?"

"Unfortunately," Momma said. "There are many not-so-pleasant parts when it comes to being a woman. I wish you didn't have to know about them."

"Like puberty and babies and stuff?"

"Yeah, and other stuff, too." Momma placed her palms flat on the tabletop and pushed herself upright. "I'm going to go to the salad bar. Want anything?"

"Black olives," I said. "And a cup of ranch dressing."

"You and those darn olives." Momma chuckled. "I'll be right back."

A warm, honey feeling spread over my chest as I watched Momma walk to the salad bar and begin to fill a plate with greens and tomatoes and cucumbers. I knew that even with my free pizza certificate and her salad bar coupon, dinner out at a restaurant would be a big hit to her wallet. Hopefully, by quitting dance and pageant stuff, she wouldn't have to worry so much about paying for things anymore.

Momma returned to the table with her salad and a few minutes later, my personal pan pizza was placed before me. I inhaled the heady, yeasty aroma of the pizza dough, already anticipating how my favorite pizza would taste when the pull of something familiar dug at my chest.

Look.

The same voice from earlier that day whispered in my ear and caused me to turn my head toward the window. I was so hungry, and all I wanted to do was eat my pizza, but something wouldn't let me. Something made me gaze out into those creepy, dark woods beyond the restaurant.

Look.

I blinked and stared out the window into the night toward a cluster of palmetto bushes by the dumpsters. My heart skipped a beat as the flashing eyes stared back at me again. Only this time, it wasn't just eyes, but a human form watching. The form rose up, those eyes never leaving my own as I recognized the familiar shape of my arms and body and legs shrouded in darkness. A shadow girl. I swallowed; my body glued to the Pizza Hut booth as my frozen limbs refused to move.

Soon.

I forced my neck to turn and looked at Momma to see if she noticed the eyes, too. She happily stabbed at a bite of salad, oblivious to the gut-punching terror that wracked my body.

Momma lifted the fork to her mouth and gave me a funny sort of look. "Everything okay, Tiff?"

I shook my head and glanced back toward the dumpsters. The shadow girl with flashing eyes was gone.

Chapter Seven

I couldn't get to sleep the night before the pageant. Worry worms wriggled beneath my skin, and the sick feeling in my stomach churned acid up my throat. My hard-earned personal pan pizza sat inside of me like a rock, and I spent half the night in bed sitting up with mushroom-flavored burps. I considered trying to make myself puke or faking sick like Ferris Bueller, but I knew that would be lying. I wanted to find some way to avoid performing in the pageant the following day, but there didn't seem to be a good answer. I had to suck it up for just one more day and then it would be over.

The purple and black alarm clock on my side table read 3:29 A.M. when I finally got out of bed. I yawned and walked to the kitchen to grab a cup of milk, hoping it would stop the burning sensation in my chest and throat. I poured myself a tall glass, downed it, and was about to go back to bed when I heard the sound. It was soft at first, kind of like the noise a puppy might make when they're panting. Then the breathing got faster and louder. Raspy wet noises gurgled into the air as I walked the few steps from the kitchen to the living room where my mother was laying in her usual spot on the couch. Panic curdled the milk in my guts as I realized the tortured, wet breathing was coming from my mother.

I padded over toward the couch on unsteady legs. As I got closer to my momma, fear gripped my lungs, making it impossible for me to breathe. I didn't know if she was having a nightmare or if she was dying, but the sounds coming from her were something awful. The panting became even more furious, and for a minute, I thought maybe she was even growling. The lights from the Christmas tree shone down on her beautiful, twisted features in a splash of red and green and blue and gold. The worst thing in the world would be for something bad to happen to my Momma and seeing her like that scared me in a way that I had never experienced before. I couldn't let my fear hold me back, though. I reached out and grabbed her arm, her skin hot to the touch as a trickle of foamy spittle spilled out the side of her mouth.

"Momma?" I tugged at her arm.

Her eyes flashed open, and I mean they *flashed*. I blinked as her lashes fluttered, all golden underneath the lids. I don't know if it was the reflection of the Christmas lights or my imagination or what, but seeing her eyes look like that sent a shiver down my spine. But what happened next was even worse. Momma stopped breathing and her body went limp. I let out a wail, grabbed her by the shoulders, and shook.

"Momma, *wake up*!"

Her eyes opened again, and she gasped. I let out a relieved breath, my whole body covered in goosebumps. She pushed herself up into a sitting position as I wrapped my arms around her neck.

"Tiffany! What's going on?"

"You were *shaking*!" Tears blurred my vision as I struggled to speak around the frog in my throat. "I thought you were gonna *die*!"

"Oh, Tiff!" Momma hugged me tight. "I'm so sorry I scared you."

"Do you need to go to the doctor?"

Momma coughed, cleared her throat, and reached for a glass of water on the coffee table. She gulped the entire glass down in a second, as if she had been hiking in a desert all day. She wiped the corner of her mouth and made an "ahh" noise of satisfaction.

"No, baby. I feel fine."

"Are you sure? What if you need medicine for seizures, or..."

"Tiff, you know it's too expensive for me to go to the doctor." Momma stood up and put a hand on my shoulder. "I know I scared you, but I promise I'm alright. I get spells like that sometimes. It looks scarier than it really is."

"Do you promise you'll go to the doctor if it happens again?" I squinted my eyes and glanced up at her in the dark. I already knew the answer. I don't think I remembered Momma going to the doctor once in my entire life. She nodded. "Sure, baby. I will. Now you need to get back to bed. Big day tomorrow."

"We don't have to go, you know," I said. "If you're feeling sick, we can just stay home and watch the Garfield Christmas special, and make cookies and..."

"There will be plenty of time for that still," Momma said. "Don't worry. We'll get into full Christmas mode after the pageant."

"Okay." I hopped back into my bed and pulled the covers up. Momma tucked me in tight, just like she used to do when I was little, and kissed me on the forehead.

"Love you, Tiffy-bear."

"Love you too, Momma."

She walked out of my room and closed the door behind her. I glanced at the clock on my nightstand. It was only 3:35 A.M.. I wished Momma had left the door open so I could hear if she had another fit again. I wished that I could just skip the pageant altogether. I lay in bed staring at my *90210* poster for I don't know how long until my eyes got tired and I only knew the black silence of sleep again.

"Okay, you got your dance bag all ready. Did you put the curling iron in there?" Momma propped her hands on her hips and gave me an impatient look the following morning. She was dressed in her silky fabric, bright pink and blue tracksuit, and white high-top sneakers. Momma liked to be able to move fast on pageant days in case any of the other parents needed help getting their girls ready to go on stage.

"Yep." I yawned and slipped into the fuzzy slippers I wore for pageants and recitals. "I've got it."

"Great. I've got our cooler packed with drinks and snacks for the day. Your dress and costumes are already in the car. Did you ever find the headband for your tap routine?"

"Mhmm. It's in my bag."

"I guess that's it then. You still feel good about performing in the pageant today?"

I paused. I did *not* feel good about doing the pageant. I felt just as sick as I had the night before, and I was tired on top of it. But I packed something in my bag that might make it all worthwhile. I needed to be a big girl and finish the things that I started.

I forced a smile. "Yep."

"Alright, baby. Let's roll!"

I grabbed my bags and followed Momma out the door and down the apartment complex stairs to her car, my slip-on shoes flapping behind me as I walked. I didn't bring up what had happened the night before, but the incident still stuck with me. I couldn't help it, but I was worried. Momma was the only thing I had in the whole world and the idea of losing her was unbearable. The entire drive over to the Civic Center I kept thinking back to the strange sounds Momma was making in her sleep, the heat radiating from her body, and most strange of all, the flash in her eyes. I figured I was probably just scared, and my mind was playing tricks on me. In truth, I was happy to see that Momma was still her energetic, vivacious self, but I had something new to be worried about when it came to her health.

I grabbed breakfast for us at the 7-11 while Momma gassed up the car; a pack of mini donuts and milk for me, a diet soda for Momma. This was another one of our little pageant day rituals that usually gave me comfort, but not today. I walked out of the convenience store with my breakfast in hand and glanced up at the sky as a big, dark cloud passed over the sun. I almost wished that Momma would get a flat tire, or her car would break down. Anything to prevent us from going to the pageant. Anything to make this sick feeling stop.

We arrived at the Civic Center just before noon, much later than we should have been. The parking lot was already half full of cars, and even more dark clouds had accumulated overhead. The pageant was set to start at 2 P.M. and would run until 5 P.M. when the winner would be announced. I chugged the rest of my milk as Momma parked, calculating the hours and minutes in my head until it would all be over. I decided that even if I didn't feel good, even if my heart really wasn't in it anymore,

I was going to try to do my best on stage. I had made up my mind that this was going to be goodbye for Suzy Dawn Dance Studio, the pageant circuit, all of it. I was going to give it one last shot and let my pageant days go for good.

The auditorium was buzzing as me and Momma lugged our bags to the backstage area. More decorations had been added to the lobby and the stage, and two giant Christmas trees flanked either side of the stage. My thick ballet tights swished together as we hurried past the orchestra to the backstage. I wore an oversized button-down shirt like a dress to keep from messing up my hair and makeup. I was supposed to stop drinking too, so that I wouldn't have to pee a million times and risk snagging my tights in the bathroom. My bladder pinched inside of me, and I regretted drinking my milk so fast.

The Civic Center conference room had been turned into a makeshift dressing room for the event, where most of the dancers practiced and got ready. Some of the more important dancers, like Paulina, got their own private rooms to practice in, but the rest of us had to share a space. I glanced around the room and saw Samantha at the far end, patiently letting her grandmother apply a bright red to her lips. Momma found a chair, and we made a little nest in the corner for ourselves, like we always did. There would be no hanging out in the auditorium today; the seats were reserved for family members, guests, and judges. I didn't have anyone but Momma that would be there to watch me, but that was okay. I was used to it. It would have been nice if Judy from the mall would have made it to one of my pageants, though.

I sat in the chair as Momma got to work, curling my bangs and spraying them into a perfect arc away from my forehead. Momma could have been a hairstylist if she wanted to, but she said she didn't have the temperament for it. She pinned the rest of my hair up into a bun on top of my head and added the sequined headband before starting on my makeup. I liked this part of getting ready for a pageant, the one-on-one, intimate attention from my mother. It felt good to have her take care of me and make me look nice and ready for the stage. I really had to use the bathroom, but it felt too good getting personal attention from her.

"There," Momma said, standing back to admire her work. "All finished. You're a beauty. You were already gorgeous, but now you're stage-ready."

"Oh, Momma..."

"Miranda, can we borrow your blush?"

Jennifer's stepmom snuck up behind Momma and held out an open palm. Someone always seemed to need bobby pins or hair spray or butt tape on pageant days, and Momma was always happy to help. She dug around in her makeup bag and pulled out a Revlon compact.

"Here you go."

"Thanks. Jennifer is so *pale* today. I don't know what's going on with that girl."

Momma glanced around her shoulder. Jennifer was slumped in a chair and already dressed in the group tap outfit, her expression slack with dark circles lining her eyes. "Does she need a little something to eat? We have snacks."

"She can't eat before a show. It will make her sluggish on stage," her stepmom said. "Thank you for the blush. I'll bring it right back."

"No worries." Momma and I exchanged worried glances. "Ready to get into your costume?"

I cringed. "I need to go to the bathroom."

She nodded and opened up the garment bag that held my group tap costume. "Hurry up though. Miss Suzy is going to come in here to check on everyone soon."

"Okay." I pressed my knees together and took fast, tiny steps toward the bathroom. Unlike the dressing room, the bathroom was blissfully empty as I found an open stall. I peeled off my tights and emptied my bladder, my gaze drawn to the graffiti written on the back of the stall door. Some of the things people wrote were so bad. I didn't understand why people would do that. I pulled up my tights and flushed and that's when I heard the gurgling, choking sound. I knew right away what it was and who was making the sound.

I opened the bathroom stall and stepped up to the sink at the same time as Paulina. I washed my hands, stealing glances at her in the mirror as she wiped the corner of her mouth with a wet paper towel. She was flawless. Her ballerina bun was glossy and there wasn't a hair out of place. Her makeup was perfect, and her legs and arms seemed longer and more slender than ever. I used to want to be like Paulina, but now as I watched her rinse her mouth at the sink and pat away a tear from her heavily mascara'd eyes, I only felt pity.

"What the hell are you looking at?"

Paulina's upper lip curled into a snarl as she turned her head to glare at me. Her collarbone looked so sharp. I thought about her broken, bloody toe, and how she probably just puked up whatever rice cakes or diet shake she had for breakfast. I should have felt embarrassed, or angry, but I only felt bad.

"Nothing." I sucked in a fast, quick breath through my nose, turned off the faucet, and walked out of the bathroom without drying my hands.

"Hello, and welcome to Suzy Dawn Dance Studio's thirteenth annual Pageant of Lights!"

Miss Suzy beamed as she addressed us all at the entrance to the changing room later that afternoon. Our pageant director pulled out all the stops and was dressed in a floor-length red ball gown with a fluted skirt and a heart-shaped peephole neckline. Thirty girls from the dance school patiently waited, dressed for the tap routine in matching black spandex leotards adorned with gold sequins and glitter. Another dozen or so older girls waited on the sidelines, dressed in their various ballerina and jazz costumes. Miss Tonya stood next to her dressed in a rad green and pink full bodysuit with geometric cutouts, her hair crimped and piled on top of her head in a giant ponytail. Everyone seemed to hold their breath as the room fell quiet.

"So, as you know, we have the Fort Myers News-Press here to cover the event as always, as well as a few very special guest judges. I wanted to wait to tell you all, but I just can't hold my excitement. We also have a few generous donors in the audience who have agreed to grant a special scholarship to our school as well as tonight's winner!"

A collective gasp filled the room. Pageant money was never a lot, usually just enough to cover entry fees, costumes, and classes. For me, winning money to fund the pageant lifestyle didn't matter anymore, and besides, I knew that I wasn't going to win, anyway. But for a lot of other girls in the show that night, big money would really up the stakes.

"Curtain call is in five minutes. I want big smiles, lots of energy and, most importantly, I want you all to have fun!" Miss Suzy raised her fists in the air and shook them. "Good luck, girls!"

A roar of applause filled the conference room, and my pulse quickened. This was it. Just three more times on stage, and it would all be over. I glanced across the room and met Samantha's gaze. She was still so new to the pageant circuit, and her bewildered expression stabbed me in the heart. I glanced over at Jennifer, who still looked like death despite her stepmother's aggressive application of blush. I stood up, gave my mom a hug, and lined up next to Miss Tonya as we prepared to go backstage. I couldn't freeze up or run away now.

It was showtime.

Chapter Eight

There was only one thing I loved more than dancing at the studio, and that was dancing in front of a live audience. We all huddled backstage and listened while Miss Suzy gave her opening speech, each of us hugging ourselves or holding our breath in anticipation of the big event. The air crackled with electricity as we took our marks behind the big velvet curtains. We stepped lightly into formation so as not to make too much noise with our tap shoes, and I readjusted my sequined headband for what felt like the hundredth time. Like magic, the curtains parted, and the lights came up. Electronic dance music boomed over the speakers and thirty girls in black and gold spandex began to tap in perfect synchronicity. The song promised that it would make us sweat, and by the end of the routine, we were all indeed drenched.

My cheeks hurt from smiling as we finished the opening number to thundering applause. We all nailed the routine, even little Samantha, who didn't miss her timing or forget a step or anything. We bowed and a little pang of regret wiggled its way into my heart as we shuffled off stage. I wished there was a way for me to keep this good feeling going, to keep dancing because I loved it and nothing more. Dancing charged me up and filled me with so much energy and power, I felt almost invincible.

I wanted to stay on the sidelines and watch Miss Tonya's dance routine, but Miss Suzy didn't want anyone backstage that day. Too many important people were going to be in the audience, and with the new prize money announcement, there was even more on the line than usual. When I got back to the dressing room, I almost forgot about my disappointment at not being able to watch my favorite dance teacher on stage. My heart leapt to my throat as I came upon my mother face-to-face with Jennifer's stepmom.

"She is *fine*. Mind your own business!"

"She is *not* fine, Janelle," Momma said. "Look at her! She can barely keep her eyes open!"

I glanced over at Jennifer, who had collapsed into a nearby chair. She was even sweatier than I was, and her eyes were half closed. She almost looked dead.

"She's a little girl! She needs more than rice cakes and water to survive." Momma squared up her shoulders. "I'm sorry but I have to speak up on this. I can't just sit back and watch these poor girls destroy themselves."

"*Right*." Jennifer's stepmom snorted. "What would you know? You're just jealous. The way your daughter eats, she'll always be too heavy for toe shoes."

CRACK.

Jennifer's stepmom gasped and brought a hand to her cheek. Everything happened so fast that I could barely register what I even saw. I glanced over at Momma and covered my mouth with my hands. Her expression scared me, and for a moment, I swore her eyes flashed as her lips pulled back over her teeth in a sneer. Momma pointed in the face of the woman she had just slapped and let out a growl.

"If you *ever* speak about my daughter, or *any* other child like that again, I'll do worse than give you a little tap on the cheek. Do we understand each other?"

Jennifer's stepmom nodded, her eyelashes furiously fluttering as she backed away from my momma. Dark yellow blooms appeared at the crotch of her white jeans as she gasped for air.

Momma chuckled low and dark as she regarded the woman's wet pants. "And drink some more water, would you? You look a little dehydrated."

I walked over to our corner as the room fell silent. The other parents huddled together and murmured to each other in hushed tones. I couldn't believe what I had just seen. Part of me wanted to get the heck out of there, but an even bigger part of me was proud as hell of my momma. I reached out to her for a hug.

"What happened?"

"Hey, baby. I'm sorry you had to see that," Momma said, wrapping me in her arms. "Some people just need to be put in their place."

"Are you gonna get in trouble?" I glanced up at her, my arms still wrapped around her waist.

Momma shook her head and glared at the other parents. "No. They know I'm right."

I squeezed her tight and sighed. I caught little Samantha's gaze from across the room. Momma released me from her hug and let out a sigh, too. "How did the tap routine go?"

"Fine," I said. "Can I go check on Sammy?"

"Yeah, just come back soon. We need to get you out of that costume."

"Okay." I picked up a juice box and a bag of chips from our cooler and brought them to Samantha. She looked even sadder than ever as I sat down next to her.

"Hey."

"Hey."

I gazed down at Sammy's slim upper arm as she sat curled into a ball against the wall. Three oval bruises stood out on her fair skin, obvious next to her dance costume. I pointed at the bruises, worried that I had caused them. "Did I hurt your arm? You know, yesterday. During the accident."

Sammy shook her head. "No. My uncle. He squeezes too hard sometimes."

"Was he rough housing with you?" I asked, my gaze trailing toward her left eye. Either Sammy's grandmother was crappy at applying eyeshadow or she had a bruise there too.

"No. He's just mean. Meaner than my grandma or Miss Suzy even. I hate him."

"I'm sorry." I wanted to comfort her. I wanted to wrap her up in a big hug and make all of it go away. "Want a snack?"

She shook her head. "No, thanks."

"Where's your grandma?"

"She went out to get cigarettes," she said. "I can't find my baton."

"Oh, no."

She glanced up at me, her eyes rimmed in red. "Can I tell you something?"

"What is it?"

"I made that stage light fall."

"Yesterday?" I frowned. "How?"

"With my mind," she said. "I looked up at it and somehow I knew that the light was loose, so I concentrated real hard and made it fall."

"How? Why would you do something like that? You could have been killed!"

Samantha shrugged. "I don't care. I just wanted all of this to stop. I don't want to do pageants and I don't want to live with my grandma anymore."

"Oh, Sammy," I wrapped my arms around her shoulder. "Maybe you can come to live with me and my momma. We have a small apartment, but I'll share my room with you."

"Thanks. I don't think that's allowed, though."

I sat there with her for a moment and shared the weight of the air. This was heavy stuff, and I didn't know what to say or do for my little friend to help make her feel better except for just being there. We watched the other girls get out of their tap costumes and get ready as though nothing happened between my Momma and Jennifer's stepmom. In truth, what she said stung a little. I knew I was a little chunky, and that I didn't look like a dancer, but it never really bothered me. Still, to hear the words come from a grown-up made my heart hurt. Seeing Momma slap that lady for saying mean things about me felt good, though.

Samantha's grandma returned, and I scooted back to where me and Momma were set up to have my lunch. She helped me into my green dress, and I ate a sandwich as Momma worked on my hair. I glanced down at my bag, more certain than ever about what I was going to do. When Momma was finished, I picked up my gym bag and noted the time. It was almost 3:00 P.M. and I was set to go on stage to sing in half an hour.

"I need to go ask Miss Tonya something," I told Momma. "I'll be right back."

"Okay, baby. Just pay attention to the time."

"I will."

I pushed past Paulina and her big, dumb tutu and fast-walked out the door of the conference room. The guy that ran the audio during our pageants was Miss Tonya's boyfriend, a cool guy named Rick who worked with musicians. He had a mustache, and I thought he was kind of cute, but nowhere near as cute as Jason Priestly.

I climbed the stairs to the sound booth and opened the door. Rick was in the darkened room, hovering over a soundboard, his eyes glued to the stage. His head whipped around when I opened the door, letting in a flood of light from the hallway.

"Shut that door, quick!"

"Sorry!" I whispered, closing the door behind me. "I, uh... they sent me up here because there's been a change."

"What kind of change?"

Rick remained focused on the soundboard and didn't even glance over at me. I padded over to his side and slid the cassette tape and a folded program across the desk. "Miss Tonya said to play this for my routine instead."

I glanced down over his shoulder at the stage from his bird's nest view. An older girl was singing *God Bless the U.S.A.* and wore a floor-length gown in red, white, and blue glitter topped with a matching cowboy hat. She was pretty, and her voice was okay, but not great. Still, I thought she was brave to sing in front of all those people.

"Oh? Tonya said that?" Rick glanced down and picked up the cassette. "What's your name?"

"Tiffany," I smiled. "Tiffany Baldwin. My musical number for the talent portion is being changed."

"Okay, kiddo. You got it," he said. "Hey, will you ask Tonya to bring me a coffee when you get a sec?"

"Sure."

"Thanks."

I spun on my heels and allowed a little fist pump in the air. My brain buzzed with electricity as I let myself out of the sound booth. It worked, but I didn't want to stick around and jinx anything. I clasped my hand over my mouth and stifled a scream as I walked back to the dressing room as fast as my feet would take me.

Chapter Nine

No one seemed to bat an eye as I returned to the dressing room, though inside, I felt like I was walking next to a fire. Everything was suddenly hot and crystal clear, and something like a jolt of lightning surged through me. I felt powerful and charged up, riding high on my little victory. Rick was going to play my backup cassette of *Jingle Bell Rock,* and no one was going to stop me from performing my routine my way.

I clutched my gym bag as I sat in the chair and let Momma give me one last touch up. She misted another layer of hairspray on my bangs to make sure they stayed in a perfect wave, then moved on to makeup. I had nearly wiped all of my lipstick off, but she didn't seem to notice or mind.

"Why do you have your gym bag?" Momma glanced up at the clock over the dressing room door as she retouched my lip color. I was nervous as heck, and it was nearly time for me to get backstage and be on deck for my talent portion of the pageant. I needed to be ready to go, and the final touches of my costume were hidden away in my bag. I couldn't tell her that, of course. It would ruin the surprise.

"Miss Tonya asked me to bring her something," I said, immediately feeling bad for lying to my momma. "I won't lose my bag. Promise."

"Okay, just make sure it's out of the way. I wouldn't want anyone to trip on it and get hurt," she said. "Good luck, baby."

"Thanks, Momma."

She pecked me on the cheek, and I sped out the door toward the stage. Parents were expressly forbidden to be anywhere near backstage during pageants, something I never understood. Miss Suzy just didn't like it. I hated that Momma had to stand all the way at the back of the auditorium to watch me. However, on this particular day, I was happy to be able to go backstage and do what I needed to do practically unnoticed.

Paulina was scheduled to perform right after me, so of course, Miss Suzy was busy in one of the rehearsal rooms watching her stretch and practice. Paulina was probably going to win the pageant. I could always tell who would win because Miss Suzy gave them the most attention and usually was the meanest to them. I wasn't sure if I felt bad for Paulina or not, but I did know one thing; I didn't want to end up like her.

I walked to the backstage area with my heart in my throat, just waiting for someone to stop me and figure out my plan, but no one did. Miss Tonya was the only adult allowed backstage to help keep the girls on-deck in line and ready to go on their marks. She looked up at me from her clipboard as I got in line behind a girl in a red and green leotard who was doing a gymnastic routine. A pang of guilt punched me in the gut as she smiled at me. She probably wouldn't be so nice to me anymore if she knew that I used her to lie to Rick.

"Ready to go, Tiffany?"

"Mhmm." I said. "Just about."

"I have to pee like a racehorse," Miss Tonya grumbled. "Miss Suzy needs to hurry the heck up."

The audience erupted in applause. A girl with a flute left the stage and whizzed past us.

"Good job, Jasmine," Miss Tonya said. She tapped the girl in the leotard on the shoulder. "Gina, you're up."

I remembered Gina's tumbling routine from practice. It was pretty good, but the music she picked was kinda boring. Gina took her place on stage and Miss Tonya glanced back at me with a pinched expression.

"Tiff, could you hold down the fort for me while I go to the bathroom? Miss Suzy is busy with Paulina, and I'm gonna pee my pants if I wait much longer."

"No problem," I said, taking the clipboard. "Don't rush. I'll know to go on when it's my turn."

"Awesome. That's why you're my favorite." Miss Tonya squeezed my shoulder and rushed past me. "I'll be right back."

Her favorite. The words stuck in me, all soft and hard at the same time. I wasn't gonna be her favorite for much longer. Miss Suzy was sure to ream her out after my performance, something I definitely felt guilty about. Still, I couldn't believe my luck. With Miss Tonya out of the way, there was nothing stopping me from performing my routine.

I knew that I had exactly three minutes to get ready before it would be my turn to go on stage, so I had no time to waste. I placed the clipboard on a nearby music stand, opened up my bag, and pulled out my tap shoes. I slipped the tap shoes on my feet, tied the laces tight, and pulled out my homemade Christmas tree costume. I had been working on the costume all month using felt, hot glue, sequins, and garland to create a wearable Christmas tree suit. I slipped the stiff, pine tree-shaped costume over my head and rummaged around in my bag for the finishing touch; a gold headband with a star sticking straight up to heaven.

Gina's music faded, and I prepared myself at the edge of the stage as the crowd cheered. I crossed my fingers and hoped that Rick still changed out my music, even if he didn't get the coffee that he was promised. Gina rushed past me in a blur of red and green and the lights lowered. This was it. My big moment. My last time performing in front of a live audience.

I grabbed the cordless microphone and positioned myself center-stage as my heart hammered away in my chest. I had practiced this routine so many times alone in my bedroom, but never had a chance to do it on stage. I bit the inside of my cheek and forced a smile as the lights flooded the stage and the first chords of *Jingle Bell Rock* floated through the air.

I sang. I tapped. I worked that stage in my Christmas tree costume as though I were a contestant on *Star Search*. As if my life depended on it. Because, whether I knew it or not, my life *did* depend on it. This was my moment, and I grabbed it by the glittery horns. I finished my entire choreographed song and dance, and no one was there to stop me. When I was finished, the audience cheered just as long and loud as they did for everyone else. My chest swelled with pride as I curtseyed and spank-stepped my way off stage to accept my fate. At that moment, I didn't care what kind of trouble I would get in. Whatever music I had to face; it was worth it.

"Tiffany! What did you do?" Miss Tonya met me as I walked offstage, her expression a mixture of wonder and worry.

Paulina waited in the wings, smirking. "Miss Suzy is going to *kill* you."

"Can it, Paulina," Miss Tonya hissed. "You're gonna miss your call."

"Piss off, Tonya." Paulina blew Miss Tonya a kiss that ended in a middle finger. I would have been scandalized by such a vulgar display if

I wasn't high on a power trip from finishing my routine.

"Yeah, Paulina," I said. "Fuck off!"

A surge of adrenaline coursed through me, and the center of my forehead began to buzz. I let out a high-pitched laugh that sounded kinda crazy. "Hahahaha! Fuck off!"

"Tiffany, let's go find your momma," Miss Tonya said. Her face was all twisted up as she led me away.

Paulina wore an equally horrified expression as she tiptoed on stage. Miss Tonya wrapped an arm around my shoulder as she guided me toward the conference room, but Momma was already one step ahead and met us in the hall.

"Tiffy! Oh, my word, you were amazing!" Momma held up her hands in anticipation of a double high-five. I slapped her palms with more force than I intended, still high on my performance. "How did you do that?"

I turned to Miss Tonya and winced. "I tricked Rick into playing the wrong music. I'm sorry."

"Oh my," Miss Tonya said. "Well, thank you for being honest, at least."

"And I told Paulina to fuck off."

"Language, Tiffany!" Momma said, the hint of a smirk at the corner of her mouth. "Come on now, we need to get you back to the dressing room before Miss Suzy has your hide."

Paulina's music for *Sleeping Beauty* sounded softly in the background as Momma helped me out of my Christmas tree costume. Just as I was slipping out of my tap shoes and into my flats, Paulina's music stopped and the muffled sound of the audience collectively gasping made my ears perk up. Momma and I exchanged a worried look and rushed out of the changing room toward the back of the auditorium.

The audience was a wriggling sea of murmuring faces when we burst in through the side door. Miss Tonya and Miss Suzy were both on stage by the time we got to the auditorium. Paulina lay in a heap in the center spotlight, wailing and grasping at her ankle.

"Kill the lights!" Miss Suzy yelled, pointing to Rick in the sound booth.

But it was too late. Everyone could see what had happened to Paulina. Red rivers of blood gushed from her toe shoe in arcs, spraying up her white tights and onto her tutu and the bodice of her costume. She clutched her knee as she howled, her beautiful, perfect features contorted in pain. Even through her thick ballet tights, it was obvious that her ankle was turned all the way around in an unnatural 180-degree angle.

"Oh, my goodness." Momma reached over and tried to cover my eyes with her hands. I pushed them away and smiled.

"Miss Suzy is so *mad*," I said, almost gleefully.

It was true. Miss Suzy wasn't worried about Paulina at all. I could hear every word she was whispering to Miss Tonya crystal clear, as though she were hissing right in my ears.

She's fucking up everything! Get her off the stage! This is such an embarrassment.

"Awesome!" A machine gun laugh ripped from my throat. The center of my forehead was tingling again. Sparkles ran through my body like lightning.

"Tiffany!" Momma glanced down at me; her eyes open wide.

"Miss Suzy is being so mean," I said, shaking my head. "She *deserves* to be embarrassed."

"Wait, you can hear them too?" Momma grabbed my shoulders, her eyes flashing.

I nodded. "Yeah."

Just then, little Samantha wandered onto the stage holding her baton, a confused expression playing out on her face. She wore a little gold crop top and a tutu, exposing way more skin than Momma would have ever let me on stage. I forgot that Samantha was supposed to go on after Paulina.

Get off the stage!

Miss Suzy placed her hand on Samantha's chest and pushed her toward the backstage area, but she didn't move out of the way. Instead, Samantha fell right on her butt and began to cry.

"Goddammit, Samantha!" A familiar voice sounded over my shoulder, followed by the smell of cigarettes. I turned to see the man who picked Samantha up from dance class the other night standing right behind Momma and me. "That fuckin' kid can't do nothin' right."

Something flipped inside my brain at that moment as I remembered the bruises on Sammy's arm. You know how you have to snap and shake a glow stick to activate the chemicals inside to make it glow? It was like that. All of a sudden, my brain felt like it was a shining neon light. My forehead was buzzing so hard the inside of my skull felt like it was on fire and all I saw was red, red, red. I stared up at Samantha's uncle and knew that I wanted him dead. I felt all my blood bubbling like a witch's cauldron, all hot and gooey under my skin. I hated him so much and I pushed that hatred through my eyeballs and shot it right back at him.

POP.

A woman screamed as something warm and wet splashed my face. I closed my eyes and the buzzing in my forehead stopped, but rivers of lava still flowed beneath my skin. I took a deep breath and opened my eyes again. The headless body of Samantha's uncle swayed; an exploded stump of skin and gore where his neck used to be. I picked at a chunk of scalp that had landed on my shoulder as his legs and torso crumpled to the floor.

Chapter Ten

Being covered in blood doesn't feel like you think it might. It's sticky and thick and just... gross. I tried not to think about the chunks of brain from Sammy's uncle that were surely stuck in my hair as a wave of bodies crashed toward the Civic Center exit. I wiped a layer of mushy skin and blood from my brow as my focus tightened like a laser beam. Grown-ups dressed in sparkling gowns and suits with ties and jackets scrambled, clawing at each other and screaming their way out of the auditorium. The lights over the stage snapped and popped as sparks flew everywhere. The scent of burning plastic and fried electrical wires filled the air. It was glorious and horrifying all at once.

Power flowed through my arms and legs from the tips of my fingers right down to my toes, just like when I performed *Jingle Bell Rock*. At that moment, I wanted to burn it all down. I wanted to blast apart all of their heads like rotten pumpkins, make them all pay for sitting back and watching while Samantha and me and even Paulina got hurt. The grown-ups did *nothing*. All of them cheered and celebrated the fact that we had to dress in scantily clad costumes, starve ourselves, and perform when we didn't want to. It was no less than what they deserved.

"Tiffany!"

Momma took me by the shoulder and shook me. The glow stick in my brain snapped again and all the hot, churning anger bubbling beneath my skin subsided. The flash flood of rage that flowed through my body ceased as I glanced up at my momma and came back down to Earth. Her beautiful face was covered in blood and brains too, and I started to cry.

"Momma?"

"Oh, my sweet baby. I'm so sorry," Momma wailed and held me to her chest. "I can't believe I let this happen."

I glanced up at the stage as the last person in the auditorium ran by us in a blur. Miss Tonya and Miss Suzy were both gone; they probably ran out the door screaming too. Paulina lay in a heap of bloody tulle in the center of the stage and looked like she was dead. Samantha's grandmother had climbed onto the stage and was tugging at her arm, trying to force her to leave. Even from clear across the auditorium, I could see Samantha's eyes flash golden green. The buzzing sensation in my forehead returned, and I knew that my little friend was in danger.

Momma followed my gaze and gasped. "Samantha."

"We gotta help her," I said. "Before it's too la—"

POP.

Samantha was painted red as her grandmother's head burst. Bodily fluids trailed down the front of her gold and white costume in chunky ribbons as she shook free from her death grip. Her grandmother's headless body hit the stage with a soft thud. Samantha unceremoniously stepped over the corpse and disappeared backstage.

Momma let out a strangled sort of yelp and grabbed my hand as we exited the auditorium toward the backstage. Despite all the chaos that was going on, for the first time, I could finally see everything a little more clearly now, kinda like that song we had to sing in chorus. But the rain wasn't gone. There were still obstacles in my way. The upbeat song turned over and over in my head as Momma and I searched for Samantha. Whatever was happening to me was happening to her too, and for whatever reason, Momma didn't seem scared. She almost seemed to understand and moved with the confidence of someone that knew exactly what to do in a completely messed up situation. But that was my momma. She always knew what to do.

The back hallways leading to the stage were empty as we continued our search for Samantha. I wanted to wipe the yuck off her face and squeeze her tight, tell her everything was gonna be okay. I knew it would be a lie, but still, she was all alone in the world now, even more alone than Momma and me. We were almost to the stage area and there was still no sign of Samantha. But we ran into someone else first.

"*You.*"

Miss Suzy stood under the harsh fluorescent lights, her eyeballs wild and popping out of her skull like in a cartoon. Her hair had gone flat on one side and black streaks of mascara trailed down her cheeks from her lashes. Her sparkly ball gown was torn at the knee, and she was barefoot, but the thing that I noticed the most was the fire extinguisher in her trembling hands.

"Move outta the way, Suzanne." Momma squeezed my hand. "Let us through."

"I know I shouldn't have taken pity on you and your freak daughter." Spittle flew from Miss Suzy's lips at the word *freak*. My blood got all bubbly again. Miss Suzy's shoulders shook as she turned on the water- works. Tears flowed from her eyes as she let out a wail. "You've ruined *everything*!"

"I'm only going to say it one more time," Momma said, her voice calm and terrifying all at once. "*Move.*"

"*Ruuuaaaa*!" Miss Suzy let out a weird sort of roar, raised the fire extinguisher over her head, and ran at full speed toward Momma and me. She didn't get very far, though.

POP.

An explosion of sequins, skin, hair, and blood splashed the ceiling, walls, and floor as Miss Suzy's body exploded. Not just her head — her *entire* body. The fire extinguisher fell with a loud *clang* as pieces of my dance teacher dripped from the light fixture overhead. My pulse slammed in my neck as I realized that this time, I didn't have a headache. I didn't feel a buzz in my forehead. I wasn't the one who made Miss Suzy burst like a bloody human balloon. I glanced up at my Momma and all the breath was sucked out of me as she returned my gaze with glowing golden eyes.

"She had it comin,'" Momma turned her head to the side, cracked her neck, and threw her shoulders back. "Come on, baby. We gotta find Samantha. Watch your step. Don't slip on that blood."

I stepped over what was left of Miss Suzy and followed my Momma down the hall. Little Samantha was sitting on the steps that led to the backstage area, curled up in a ball and crying. Momma scooped her up into her arms and Samantha clung to her like a baby monkey.

"It's okay, sweetie. Let's go get you cleaned up." Momma hitched Samantha on her hip with one hand and held on to me with the other as she walked back up the stairs. "We can't go out the front. We'll need to find another way."

Momma walked us through the darkened backstage area toward a glowing red EXIT sign. Momma's eyes were still shining bright as a flashlight, giving us all the light we needed to make our way through. Before we reached the door, Momma and I both heard a whimper that made us whip our heads all the way around.

"Please don't kill me!" Miss Tonya was crouched down in a corner of the stage, clutching her purse. Panic leapt up in my chest as I sensed Momma get all hot and bubbly again.

"Don't hurt her, Momma!" I begged. "Miss Tonya is one of the good ones!"

"Keys." Momma let go of my hand and held out a palm in her direction.

Miss Tonya plunged a hand down into her purse and brought up a set of keys with a shaky hand. "They're Rick's. He's got the black pickup truck with the Metallica sticker on it."

"Of course he does," Momma said, taking the keys. "Tell anyone you saw us, and I'll come back and turn you into confetti, you got that sweetie?"

Miss Tonya sobbed and nodded.

Momma brushed past her with little Samantha still clinging to her side. I let out a sigh and waved to my favorite dance teacher for the last time. "Bye, Miss Tonya. Sorry about the pageant."

Momma pushed open the door leading to the back of the building. The sun hung low in the sky and a blast of cold, wintry air chilled the still wet blood on my hair and cheeks. Rick's black pickup shone like a getaway beacon at the far end of the parking lot as me and Momma broke into a jog. She opened the passenger side door of the truck and stuffed Samantha into the middle. I climbed in next to her as Momma went around the front and slid behind the wheel. She jammed the key into the ignition and Rick's truck rumbled to life as loud, heavy metal music blasted from the speakers. Momma threw the truck into reverse and headed out onto US-41 into the sunset.

"Is she still sleeping? We're gonna have to stop soon and get gas." Momma ruffled Samantha's hair as I shifted in the passenger seat. I pulled the denim jacket we found in the car up over Samantha's blood-stained shoulders as she dozed at my side.

"I think so," I said. "Wake up, Sammy. We're gonna get out soon."

"Let her sleep a minute longer," Momma said.

The roads were pitch black as we drove Rick's car late into the night. I don't know how far Momma got away from town and the Civic Center and everything that had happened, but I knew it was very late. As we drove away from town, I half expected police sirens and flashing lights to follow us and make us pull over, but that never happened. Momma and I didn't talk the whole way, probably because we were both in shock. Now that I had time to process everything, I was ready to ask some questions.

"So, did you always know that I could do... that?"

"Do what, sweetie?"

"*Momma*," I said, giving her a look. "You're not gonna make me say it, are you?"

"Did I always know that you could make people explode? No. I hoped you wouldn't be able to, at least."

"Have you always been able to do it?"

Momma pursed her lips and nodded. "Mhmm. I've spent a long time trying to get it under control."

"Why didn't you tell me?"

Momma shrugged. "I dunno. I guess I hoped that you wouldn't turn out like me. I wanted you to grow up normal, have a normal life. It isn't easy to be this way."

"I think it's kind of awesome."

"It's not. Someday, you'll see. You already know how hard it is to control. Sometimes you accidentally hurt the people you love the most." She held her breath and paused before beginning again.

"Did you hurt someone you loved?"

A tear trailed down Momma's cheek.

"I loved your Daddy. I just want you to know that."

I sat with her words for a minute as the exit to Gainesville passed us by. Finally, when my heart stopped beating in my ears, I took a long, slow breath and asked my Momma the question I had been wondering about my whole life.

"What happened to my dad? Tell me the truth."

Momma sniffed and glanced up at the rearview mirror. She cleared her throat and wiped her cheek.

"When you were six months old, your daddy lost his job and his momma died all in the same week. He got really depressed. Started drinking every night. He even got a little rough with me a couple of times. I let things build up, and I was so young. I didn't ask anyone for help or tell anyone what was going on."

"Go on."

"Well, one day he started drinking real early. He was sitting on the bed, but he wasn't there anymore. Like the thing that made him who he was had gone away. There was no more light behind his eyes. I went to the bathroom and when I came out, you were crying in your crib, and he was standing over you shouting for you to be quiet and all sorts of other awful things. That's when it happened."

"You made his head explode?"

Momma didn't say anything and just kept driving. I stayed quiet too, digesting everything she had just confessed. The next exit sign passed before she finally spoke again.

"I didn't know what else to do, so I cleaned you off and we've been on the run ever since." Momma sniffed again, reached across Samantha and gave my hand a squeeze. "I'm sorry I never told you the truth. I'm sorry that we're like this. I'm so sorry, baby."

I squeezed her hand back. "Weren't you afraid that you might hurt me, too?"

Momma let out a sob and squeezed the steering wheel. "No. Never. I would make the entire world explode before I ever hurt you."

"That's what happened to my mom and dad." Samantha yawned and sat up in her seat. "When I was a baby."

"Sammy!" I wrapped my arm around her shoulders and pulled her in for a hug. "What? No! You couldn't have done something like that."

"Grandma didn't want me to know, but my uncle told me," she said, her voice still sleepy. "He said when I was a baby, someone came into our trailer and blasted them both in the head with a shotgun. The police never found any bullets, though."

"Oh, Samantha." Momma said. "That's awful."

"I always knew it was me, though," she said. "I knew I was the one who did it. I always knew that I was bad, just like my grandma said."

"It doesn't mean you're a bad person," Momma said. "We're just different. That's all."

"Where are we going?" Samantha asked. "I'm hungry."

"We're going to get some gas, and then we'll get some food and I'll try to find somewhere safe to stay tonight," Momma said. "Would you like to live with us now, Samantha?"

Samantha glanced at me and nodded. "Yeah."

I smiled. I always wanted a little sister.

Momma pulled off the interstate toward a 24-hour gas station. My stomach rumbled. I was getting hungry, too. She pulled up to a pump, turned off the engine to Rick's truck and gave me a weary sort of look.

"Where are we gonna live now, Momma?" I asked. "What are we gonna do?"

Momma sighed and gazed out the windshield toward a vast, vacant field. "I dunno. How about Tennessee?"

"The mountains?"

"Yeah. We can get us one of them little cabins and live in the woods," Momma said. "How's that sound?"

"I'd like that."

"I gotta pee," Samantha moaned.

"Me too." I glanced at Momma. We were all still covered in blood and in no state to go inside a gas station. "Should I take Sammy to the field?"

"Yeah, just be quick. I'll watch from here."

"Come on, Sammy. We gotta go pee in the field, camping style."

"Okay."

I took Sammy's hand and helped her out of the car and into the night. We walked over to the field, squatted, and relieved ourselves. I kept my eyes on Momma the whole time, and my heart filled up with love for her all over again. Part of me was scared, but part of me finally felt whole again, too. I knew that no matter what, me and Momma would take care of each other and figure out a way to get by. We always did.

When Samantha was finished peeing, she hiked up her tights and took my hand again. I was still sad for Samantha, but glad that she was going to be part of our family now. She was a nice little girl, and she deserved better than what life had given her. I would be glad to share my momma's love with her. I closed my eyes and made a wish. Christmas was coming, and I didn't need new roller skates or unicorn stickers or a poster for my wall. I needed to know that we would all be okay someday. I needed a miracle.

"Hey," Samantha said, holding out her hand. "What's that?"

I opened my eyes as a flurry of something cold and wet landed on my nose. I held out my hand and laughed as a snowflake melted in the palm of my hand.

"Would you look at that, Sammy?" I said. "Snow in Florida. Dreams do come true."

Acknowledgements

This story came from my heart but was made possible because of the love, support and inspiration from so many.

Thank you to my parents, Laura and Kevin Owen for always supporting my love of reading and writing and nurturing my creativity. I love you and this book is for you.

Thank you to my husband, David, whose unwavering support of my writing career makes it possible for me to live my dream. I love you, thank you.

Thank you David, Luke, and Max for supporting your weird mom and her books. You guys are the reason for everything I do. I love you.

Thank you Teri, Jenna, Phoenix, my sisters and best friends. Life would be super boring and lonely and sad without you.

Thank you to my extended family, the Dalrymples, Owens, McPhees, and Wootens. Thank you to my many grandparents, aunts, uncles, nieces, nephews and cousins who have come out to support my writing. Thank you, thank you, thank you.

Thank you Damien Casey and Grace R. Reynolds for being my go-to author pals. Publishing is wild and I'm so grateful to have you both to collaborate and commiserate with. Thank you to the many, many author friends who have supported me and my work and who inspire me every day!

Thank you to the legion of readers, bloggers and reviewers who have constantly supported me from the beginning. Heather (Heather Renee), Madison Herrera (Madison Can Read), Kirsten Craig (Spine of Motherhood), Maddy (of Maddy's Needful Reads), Gwen (Gwen Reads Horror), Chaz, Ollie, Bon the Witch, Sam (Expert Book Smuggler), Brigitte (Brigitte Reads), Heather Jane, Laurie (Barks Books), Katrina (Xtremekatrine Reads), Erica (Erica Sniffs Books), and so many more. Your support means the world to me, thank you, thank you, a million times thank you.

Thank you Lisa Frank, R.L. Stine, Anne M. Martin, Elvira, Dolly Parton, Paula Abdul, Star Search, glitter, sequins, spandex, the color pink and Little Debbie's Zebra Cakes for making this story possible.

Thank you to the wonderful Candace Nola for your editing guidance and support. The indie horror world is better with you in it!

And lastly, thank you to my publisher, Joey Powell, for giving this story a wonderful new home.